The King of Pawleys

The King of Pawleys

David Bernstein

Alpharetta, GA

This is a work of fiction. Names, characters, businesses, places, and events are either the products of the author's imagination or are used in a fictitious manner. Any resemblance to actual persons, living or dead, or actual events is purely coincidental.

ISBN: 978-1-63183-375-5

Library of Congress Control Number: 2018946936

10 9 8 7 6 5 4 3 2 060618

Printed in the United States of America

♾This paper meets the requirements of ANSI/NISO Z39.48-1992 (Permanence of Paper)

For my family—from the original Pawleys crew to all future generations of Dads, Moms, Petes, Sammys, and Alis.

"Do any men grow up or do they only come of age?"

—Stephen King

Chapter 1

DAD TURNS THE CAR ONTO THE SOUTH Causeway and I know we're almost there. I've been excited ever since we left home, but now that we're this close, I can feel my heartbeat speeding up and goose bumps forming all over my arms. I look over at my brother to tell him where we are, but he's been asleep for the last few hours. Actually, he looks pretty funny: His head is leaning all the way over the side of his car seat, and he's holding onto his stuffed elephant like his life depends on it. But his eyes are closed peacefully as if he was at home in his bed, and his mouth is gaping wide open. I try to smile at him, but I realize that I already *am* smiling—another natural reaction to being this close, I guess. Then, all of a sudden, the trees on both sides of the road give way to marshes, and spread out in front of us is my favorite place in the whole world.

Pawleys Island.

Unable to control myself, I shout to my parents in the front seat, "We're here!"

"Yep, we're *finally* here," Dad says from the driver's seat. "Are you excited, Peter?"

"Yeah, I'm excited!" I reply. We cross over the creek, where a few people are fishing over the side of the bridge. Among them are three kids a little older than me, all with bright-blonde hair and matching red swim trunks. They look bored. All I can think is, *How can you possibly be bored here?*

I roll my window down a little as we turn onto the main road. The car instantly fills up with warm, salty air. I can hear the waves from the beach just beyond the houses to my left, and smell the pluff mud from the creek to my right. It will only be a few minutes now before I'm swimming in the ocean. I can't contain myself any longer. I start dancing in my seat, waving my hands in the air and singing, "Yeah, yeah, we're at Pawleys! Yeah, yeah, we're at Pawleys!"

I hear Mom chuckle so I keep going for a minute, but

then, out of the corner of my eye, I see my brother start to move. He's awake, and I quickly realize that between the noise from the window and my singing, it's my fault he's awake. *Uh oh.* I settle down, roll my window up, and sit quietly, fully expecting Dad to yell at me. But surprisingly, he doesn't say a word. I lean up in my seat so I can see his eyes in the rearview mirror, thinking he'll at least give me the famous you-should-have-known-better glare. But he doesn't even look back at me. Instead, his eyes look calm and relaxed, like he's in a trance, too deep in thought or lost in memories to even notice what I did. I lean back in my seat, thankful for the rare chance to avoid his discipline. Mom knows that I was spared, too, and she looks back at me with a warm smile. I smile back, and then she turns her attention to my brother.

"Good morning, Sammy!" she says. "Look where we are!"

But Sammy already knows. He's only five years old, but we've been here every summer since he was born, so he can recognize it just as easily as the rest of us. "Pawleyyys!" he answers.

"Yep, Pawleys!" Mom says. "And look! There's the rental house!"

We pull into the driveway and I unbuckle my seatbelt before the car even stops. Sammy sees me and unbuckles his, too. Now Dad's eyes meet mine in the mirror, but they're his happy eyes, and I hear him unlock the automatic doors for us. He knows what's about to happen; it's been the same every year since I can remember.

When the car finally stops, all four of us jump out at the same time. Dad pops the trunk and heads toward the back of the car, but I zoom past him and run straight for the water as fast as I can. Sammy is right on my heels. We don't stop to go inside the house, put on sunscreen, or even change into our swim trunks. We just run straight to the beach, stopping in the sand only long enough to take off our shoes and shirts, but leave our normal shorts on. Then we race into the ocean, and our week-long beach vacation officially begins.

Pawleys is a small island on the coast of South Carolina. It's only a few miles long and very skinny; in most places you can run from the beach to the creek in a matter of seconds. I've been to a few other beaches, but none of them are as great as this one. The sand is soft, the water is warm, and the waves are the perfect size for boogie-boarding, floating on rafts, and of course swimming. There are usually other kids around to play with, but it's never too crowded. At low tide you can walk on the beach and find tons of cool seashells, including super-rare Pawleys Island Shells, which aren't found anywhere in the world except here. Dolphins swim by every now and then to bring you good luck. There are crabs in the creek, but they don't bother people, and you can catch them with a little help from a grown-up. Seagulls and pelicans fly everywhere, and sandpipers run along the shoreline digging for food.

Although most of the buildings on the island are houses, there are plenty of shops and restaurants on the mainland just across the creek. But we don't go over there too often. That's because Mom and Dad like to cook the same special meals every year, and Dad always reminds us that they're the same meals he used to eat when he came here as a kid. That's pretty cool, I guess, but I don't really care about the food. All I care about is playing outside, making new friends, and enjoying my break from the boring summer nothingness back home.

As I'm swimming, I look back toward the house and see Mom and Dad on the beach, Mom picking up our stray shirts and Dad setting up some chairs in the sand. They haven't changed clothes either, but they did bring a beach bag from the car that I know contains some basic supplies: towels, sunscreen, a couple plastic shovels for us kids, and a couple of books for them. Dad, apparently over his trance, waves to get my attention and then points at his stomach. I know what this means. When no adults are in the water with us, my brother and I are only allowed to go in as deep as where the water is even with Sammy's belly button. I look over at Sammy to see if we are actually out too far, and I grin. If there were no waves, the water would easily be up to Sammy's chest. But there *are* waves, and the water always looks more shallow just before a wave breaks. I wait for the perfect time, right when a big one is just about to crash on us, and I can clearly see Sammy's waistline. I point toward my brother, give Dad a thumbs-up, and quickly turn back toward the ocean so he can't reply. Oldest trick in the book.

Chapter 2

After letting us swim for a while, Dad waved again. This time he pointed to the house; time to go in. As I made my way out of the water, I noticed a couple kids playing in the sand next door. One was a girl about my age with long, curly red hair, and the other was an older boy. They were burying their dad's legs in the sand, laughing and jumping on him every time he tried to get up. It didn't even register as unusual until Mom said something.

"It looks like the Hendersons aren't back this year," she said to Dad as we gathered our things.

And I thought this trip couldn't get any better!

The Hendersons usually rented the house next to ours for the same week we're at Pawleys. We were neighbors every summer for the last four years. That wouldn't have been a problem except that their son, Derek, was easily the biggest bully I'd ever met. He was five years older than me, at least a foot taller, and just plain mean to everybody, all the time. We actually got along really well the first year we met, which was good because Sammy was still a baby and kept Mom and Dad too busy to play with me very much. But for some reason, when I saw Derek again the next summer, he was different. At first he just said mean things and didn't want to play. But before long he was knocking over sandcastles all up and down the beach, pushing little kids for no reason, and throwing people's toys up onto the sand dunes. That one was the worst, because no one is allowed to climb on the dunes, not even grown-ups. So when he threw something up there, you had to choose between going to get it—which almost surely meant you were going to get in trouble—or just losing your toy. Last year he started calling me "Petey-Weety," which doesn't even make any sense, but I still didn't like it because I knew he was only saying it to be mean.

But now he was gone. As we started up toward the house, I looked back over at the new family playing in the sand. Just then the red-haired girl glanced toward us and our eyes met. She smiled and waved at me with a sand-coated hand.

What happened to Derek and his family? Maybe they decided to come on a different week this year. Maybe they found another beach. Maybe they moved to Switzerland. I didn't know, and I didn't care. As I smiled and waved back at our new neighbor, all I knew was that this was going to be the best week ever.

We dried off and then helped Dad unload the car. Sammy and I took our suitcases to our bedroom and unpacked. Well, *I* unpacked. All Sammy did was carefully place his stuffed elephant, named Alfonso, on his bed, then go into the kitchen and ask Mom when dinner would be ready. I heard her say "Soon," and let out a sigh as she continued unpacking the groceries we brought from home.

I heard Sammy say "Okay," and then his quick footsteps started echoing through the house as he ran from room to room, jumping up on every couch, chair, and bed he could find. I glimpsed out my bedroom doorway to see Dad emerging from his room, and as Sammy ran by, Dad grabbed him, threw him down on floor, and started tickling him. Sammy laughed hysterically. I raced out of my room and jumped on Dad's back, just as Mom grabbed Sammy's arm and tried to free him from Dad's clutches. Dad let Sammy go and took hold of me instead. He pulled me to the floor and jolted me right in the ribs, setting me into a fit of laughter as only he could do. Mom came to my rescue, too, but Dad pinned her down and tickled her feet. Then Sammy jumped on Dad's back, and the battle went on for at least ten minutes, all four of us laughing and jumping and pushing and pulling and squirming and tickling and laughing.

Dinner the first night was shrimp and grits. Mom and Dad always make a big deal out of buying fresh shrimp from the local fishermen, but I can never tell the difference from the stuff we get at home. For the rest of the week we eat at the dining-room table, but every year on the first night we take our bowls out to the front porch and sit in the rocking chairs looking out over the beach. As simple as this sounds, it's actually one of my favorite traditions. It just makes me feel completely immersed in the calm, relaxing atmosphere of this beautiful place, signaling my entire body to enter vacation mode.

My brother started to climb into Mom's lap to eat, but she stopped him and said, "Sammy, if you want to try sitting in your own chair this time, you can." His eyes lit up at the new privilege, and he quickly jumped up into the chair next to hers. His legs were wiggling with excitement as Mom handed him his bowl. He carefully scooped a bite onto his spoon and started to raise it to his mouth. But his focus was too closely locked on that one bite, and he didn't notice his shaking legs toppling his bowl until it was too late. His entire dinner fell with a crash, the bowl shattering and the food splattering all over the floor. The smile vanished from Sammy's face. He stopped wiggling, and he, Mom, and I all looked over at Dad, wondering just how bad the yelling would be.

But Dad was back in his trance, just staring out at the hypnotic waves as he slowly ate his dinner. He didn't even turn his head toward us when he calmly said, "Peter, please go get the cleaning stuff and help your brother. Be careful with the broken pieces of the bowl."

"Yes, sir," I answered. I set my bowl down and went to the kitchen to get some paper towels, some cleaning spray, and the trash can. Mom was already picking up chunks of porcelain and dropped them in the trash can when I got back to the porch. Sammy grabbed the paper towels, and the three of us had the mess cleaned up in no time.

Mom took everything back inside and returned with a new bowl for Sammy. She looked at him and whispered, "If you want to try again, you may. Just be more careful."

He smiled wide and got back in his own chair, and he didn't spill anything else for the rest of the meal.

After dinner we went for a walk on the beach. It was low tide, so we went close to the water where the sand was firm and the shells were plentiful. The breeze was strong and cool. Sammy and I ran ahead to the first jetty, which is basically a big pile of rocks that extend from the sand dunes way out into the water to break the waves before they get too big. There are jetties about every ten houses, which makes them good landmarks for walks and boundaries for games. The one closest to our house is the first one you would reach if you started at the South End and went up the beach toward the north.

When we got to the jetty, we stopped to look back at Mom and Dad. They were walking slowly about five houses behind us, holding hands and surely talking about boring grown-up stuff. Dad saw us and held his hand straight up, signaling us to stop and wait for them before climbing over the rocks and going on.

So, Sammy and I started looking at the shells nearby. A minute later, I heard some rustling from the other side of the jetty, and I looked up to see the red-haired girl from next door appear at the top and start climbing down on our side. She saw me right away and started climbing in my direction, obviously aiming to talk. My mouth felt dry and my muscles tensed up. I looked around for my brother, thinking maybe he could talk to her first, but he was too far away, ankle-deep in the water, chasing a sandpiper. For a split second I considered bolting toward Mom and Dad, but before I could do anything she hopped down right in front of me, flashed a big smile, and said "Hi!" in a warm, happy voice.

"Um, hi," I said back. It's weird, because I usually get really nervous when I meet new people, but for some reason I instantly felt relaxed and comfortable with her.

"I'm Ali. I remember seeing you earlier today. Guess you're staying next door this week?"

"Yeah, we stay in that house every year," I managed to reply.

"Cool! This is my first time here. My mom told me nobody knows about this place, so I was worried I wouldn't have anybody to play with. Well, I mean I have my big brother, but he's fifteen, so all he wants to do is walk on the beach and meet girls. We were walking together just now, but then he met some chick in a bikini and told me to go away. He called me a shrimp. I thought about whining and making a scene so the girl wouldn't like him, but instead I decided to just say 'okay' and come home and put a bunch of sand in his bedsheets. That'll teach him. Anyway, now I don't have to worry about him because I can play with you instead. You got a name?"

"Peter."

"Hmm," she said with a thoughtful look. "You look more like a 'Pete' to me."

"Nobody calls me Pete," I said, although I've never really thought about it.

"Well, somebody does now," she said definitively. "I think it suits you." Clearly there was no use arguing about it, and I didn't want to argue with this girl anyway. So that was that.

"So, what do you think of Pawley's so far?" I asked her.

"Oh, I love it. This place is magical."

Just then Sammy ran up to us. As I looked over at him, I noticed Mom and Dad out of the corner of my eye. They weren't too far away anymore. In fact, they should have been right next to us if they had kept their course on the firm sand, but for some reason they decided to walk around me at a bit of a distance. Weird. My brother drew my attention back to where we stood. "Look, Peter! I found a Pawleys Shell!"

"That's not a Pawleys Shell," I told him dryly. Looking back at Ali, I saw her face quickly turn from happy to concerned. She clearly didn't approve of my bursting Sammy's bubble. I turned back to my brother and added, "But it's still a cool shell. You should keep it and show Mom and Dad."

Ali, still not satisfied, smiled at my brother and said, "Well, it's a shell, and you found it at Pawleys, so that makes it a Pawleys Shell in my book."

He smiled big and raced off toward Mom and Dad.

"That's my brother, Sammy," I told her, then added, "You gonna give him a new name, too?"

Ali laughed out loud. "Nope," she said. "Just you."

I smiled. "Well, it looks like my parents are waiting for me. I better go."

"Okay, well have a good walk. See ya later, Pete!" And with one more flash of her smile, she took off back toward her house to sabotage her brother's bedding.

CHAPTER 3

AFTER OUR WALK, IT WAS ALREADY TIME for bed. Mom and Dad told us to go brush our teeth—another new privilege for Sammy, since they usually helped him with that—and we climbed into our twin beds. After a few minutes, Sammy whispered, "Hey Peter, what's that girl's name with the red hair?"

"Ali," I whispered back.

"I like Ali," he said. "We should play with her tomorrow."

For the second time today I felt goose bumps run down my arms. The only reply I could manage was, "Okay. Goodnight, Sammy."

"Night," he said back, and we both fell asleep fast.

I was awoken in the middle of the night by the sound of voices on the beach outside. Somebody was shouting, and they were being pretty loud if I could hear it all the way from my bedroom. I sat up and tried to look out the window, but I didn't have a good angle and all I could see was the water and the tiny sliver of the moon above. I lay back down. Other people were on vacation here, too, and although it was odd to hear such loud noises, it wasn't that unusual for people to take a late-night walk on the beach. I closed my eyes and tried to go back to sleep.

But the shouting continued, and then more voices joined in. This time I stood up and walked to the window. Sammy stirred, and in a sleepy voice he murmured, "Peter? What's going on?"

"Nothing, go back to sleep," I told him. But he opened his eyes and saw me at the window, so he got up and joined me.

We peeked down together and saw a crowd of four or five big kids arguing on the beach. It was pretty dark outside, plus everything looked blurry through my sleepy eyes, so I couldn't make out any of their faces. But I could definitely see one of the kids punch another one right in the face. That's when things got crazy. The shouting reached a whole new volume, the group became a dogpiled mess, and I saw punches and kicks and elbows flying everywhere. The fight continued for a few more moments, but the noise must have woken up more people because I saw a light come on at Ali's house. The kids looked up and a few of them ran off, but one kept attacking the guy on the sand until Ali's dad shouted, "Hey, what's going on down there?"

At that, the attacker gave the other kid one more hard kick, then took off in the opposite direction from where the others had run. The boy on the sand lay motionless. Ali's dad started down toward the beach and called out, "Brian? Brian, is that you?" His pace quickened, and he turned back toward his house and shouted, "Karen, it's Brian! Come quick!"

I saw Ali's mom sprint from the house and meet her husband on the beach, and they reached the injured boy together. I heard Ali's mom cry out as they helped him up. I could tell Ali's big brother was very badly hurt. They helped him limp back up the stairs and into the house, and all was calm again.

I looked down at Sammy. He was shaking, and tears were falling down his cheeks. "Listen, everything's okay," I told him. "His parents will take care of him, just like Mom and Dad help us when we get hurt. Let's just go back to bed."

"Okay," he said weakly, and I tucked him in and kissed

him on the forehead. Then I got back in my bed and closed my eyes, but I was far from sleep. I lay there in silence for a long time, my mind racing.

I don't remember ever going back to sleep, but I must have because the next thing I knew, it was light outside. Sammy was still asleep, Alfonso wrapped in the covers with him. I got up and went to the kitchen to find Mom and Dad already up. Mom smiled and said, "Good morning, sweetie! How did you sleep?"

"Okay," I said plainly. Dad's eyes sharpened slightly, like he knew I was holding something back. I thought about telling them what Sammy and I witnessed last night, but something made me keep quiet. I needed to change the subject. "How about y'all?"

"Good," Mom said, "but it's never quite the same when you sleep away from home, huh? I tossed and turned a good bit, but I made it. Tonight will be better."

She started cooking breakfast. Sammy came in when he smelled the bacon, and we ate a quiet, low-key meal. I kept peeking at Dad. I knew he could sense something was wrong, but he didn't press me. Instead, when we finished eating, he loudly said "Well!" and he clapped his hands once. "Who's ready to go down to the beach?"

Although I was not thrilled with the idea of visiting the scene of the crime, I *was* still on vacation, and a swim might help me forget about what I saw. We put on our swim trunks and sunscreen and went out to the porch to wait for Mom and Dad. But Dad called out to us, "You boys go on down. Mom and I are going to clean up the kitchen, and we'll be down in a few minutes. Peter, you're in charge. Just play nice with your brother, and don't go in the water until we get there."

"Yes, sir," I replied. Wow, now I was getting a new privilege! I didn't remember Pawleys being the venue for my parents to dish out so many upgrades before, but I wasn't about to complain. Sammy and I walked down the porch stairs to the beach.

The sun was bright, and the sky was blue and flawless. The sand was still cool from last night, and a gentle breeze was blowing warm air off the ocean. Sammy and I started building a sandcastle. Some time later, Mom and Dad arrived. They set up their chairs right next to where we were playing and started reading their books. Not too long after that, I decided to go for a swim to wash the sand off my legs. Sammy quickly followed. We ended up staying in the water for a while, but then something—or rather, some*one*—on the beach caught my attention. Ali and her mom had come down from their house, and they were standing right there talking to my parents. I started heading in right away, and again Sammy followed suit.

When we reached the chairs, Dad said, "Hey guys, there are towels in the beach bag." I grabbed one for myself and tossed one to my brother, and as we dried off I looked at Ali. Her face was white, her eyes were bloodshot, and her bright smile from yesterday was nowhere to be found. She had obviously been crying a lot. Her head was hanging low, but she looked up at me and I put on my best sympathetic smile. Her look quickly changed, from sad to what seemed like a little . . . confused?

Before I could say anything, Dad introduced us to Ali's mom, Mrs. Baxter. I shook her hand and told her it was nice meeting her, and Sammy did the same. Then Dad turned to me and said, "And I believe you already met Alison, huh, Peter?"

"Yes, sir, on our walk last night," I replied.

"Well, why don't you see if she wants to play with you and Sammy?"

I looked at Ali and mustered up, "Hey, do you want to dig a hole to China?" She managed a weak giggle. I grabbed the shovels from the beach bag and we set to work.

We dug in silence for a while, but we were close enough to the grown-ups to hear their conversation. They were talking about the fight last night. Ali's parents clearly had no idea who beat Brian up, or why. They said he would be fine, which I was very glad to hear, but that it would definitely be a few days before he was up and about again. When they were at the end of their talk, Ali's mom said, "Listen, I hate to impose, but is there any way y'all could keep an eye on her today while we take care of Brian? She just needs to play and try to take her mind off all this." My parents agreed, so she called over to Ali and said, "Play nice with Peter and Sammy, and listen to their parents. I'll be right inside our house if you need anything. Just try to have some fun, okay, princess?"

She nodded quietly, but when her mom turned to leave, Ali called after her. Mrs. Baxter spun around again and said, "Yes, princess?"

In a simple, matter-of-fact tone, Ali said, "Mom, it's *Pete* and Sammy. Not Peter."

Ali's mom went home and the three of us kept digging, but after a few minutes Ali suggested we go swimming. Sammy and I agreed, so the three of us went out into the water while Mom and Dad kept reading.

As soon as we were out far enough so my parents couldn't hear us, Ali faced me with an entirely new look in her eyes. She seemed shrewd, like a detective on TV that just figured out an important clue in his case. With a firm voice she said, "All right, Pete, what do you know about this?"

"About what?" I asked. I don't know why, but I didn't

want to tell her what I had seen in the night. She was clearly upset about it, and I didn't want to make her feel any worse. At that moment, I also felt bad myself—almost guilty—like I should have done something to help her brother instead of just watching.

"Pete, don't play dumb. You gave me that sympathetic smile as soon as you walked up to us, before anyone even told you what happened. Now, I've had a terrible night and morning, and my parents think there's no way to find out who did this to my brother. But I *know* I can figure it out. And I could really use your help. You come here every year, so you must know this island pretty well. Much better than I do, anyway. And you're funny and sweet, so you'll keep me from just being upset all week. But look, I know this is your vacation, so if you don't want to help, that's fine. But either way, if you know something, you better tell me!"

I felt pure self-conviction and utter defeat at the same time. Here was this girl, paying me more compliments in one minute than I've received in my entire life so far, asking for my help in a mission driven purely by love for her brother. Why on earth did I hesitate? Of course I would help.

"I heard shouting on the beach in the middle of the night," I said flatly. "It woke me up. I got up and looked out the window and . . . watched it happen."

"Tell me exactly what you saw. Every detail."

I recounted the story as best I could. It must have been difficult for her to hear, but she didn't show any sign of weakness. She just stood there in the ocean, soaking up my words like a sponge.

When I finished, she said, "Thank you for telling me that, Pete. Okay, let's back up. How many boys were there in all?"

"I really couldn't tell. It was dark and I was tired. Obviously your brother makes one, and there were three, maybe four more."

"What did they look like?"

"I'm sorry, I just don't know. It looked like they were all about the same age as your brother, but I couldn't make out any of their faces."

Sammy had been standing there listening to our entire conversation, disappearing occasionally to swim under a wave. But now he spoke up. "Peter, what are you talking about? You know who it was!"

Annoyed, I gave him an elbow to the ribs and said, "Sammy, stay out of this."

But Ali glared at me with the same disapproval as yesterday when I discounted Sammy's seashell. She then gently addressed my brother: "Sammy, did you see all of this, too?"

He nodded.

"And who do you think it was?"

Happy to have the spotlight, his chest puffed out, and with an air of authority he said, "It was Derek Henderson!"

I rolled my eyes. "Sammy, there is *no way* it was Derek. He's not here this year, remember? Now like I said, you stay out of this."

But Ali latched on, determined to follow every possible lead. "Who is Derek?" she asked. So, I told her a short version of the history between me and Pawleys Island's biggest jerk. She listened carefully. When I finished, she said, "Well, there's certainly something wrong with this Derek guy. Maybe we should keep our eyes out for him."

"Ali, I don't want to keep my eyes out for him. I'll be perfectly happy if I never see him again for the rest of my life. I know you want to follow every lead, but this is one we can go ahead and cross off the list. He's not the one who beat up your brother. He's not here. *You're staying in his house!*"

We all fell silent. The tide had come in a lot since morning, and the waves were getting pretty big. It was close to lunchtime anyway, so without another word we went back to my parents' chairs and dried off. I asked Dad if Ali could have lunch at our house, and he agreed. So we collected our toys and chairs and beach bag, and went inside.

CHAPTER 4

IT WAS HIGH TIDE AFTER LUNCH, AND the day had gotten hot, so we decided to stay inside and play UNO for a while. Mom and Dad played with us for a few games, but then they went out to the porch to relax. I took the opportunity to bring up our mission. "So Ali, how should we start looking for the kids that beat up your brother?"

Over lunch and the card game, Ali had slowly but surely started feeling better and acting more like the cheerful, radiant girl I met yesterday. She had excellent manners and was very polite to my parents, which made them like her instantly. And she continued to befriend Sammy, quickly becoming a hero in his eyes by coming to his aid any time I slighted him.

But at the mention of her brother, her smile disappeared and she put her cards down. "I think we should start by walking up and down the beach this afternoon," she said. "You said all of the kids involved were about Brian's age. So, let's just look around for a group of boys that are a little older than us. From what I've seen, there can't be too many here."

"Good idea!" Sammy said. "I bet if we ask, Mom and Dad will let us go for a walk by ourselves."

I opened my mouth to dismiss the idea, but before I could say anything Ali jumped in. "Perfect! Good thinking, Sammy. Why don't you go ask them?" He smiled big and hurried toward the porch. Ali watched him off, but as soon as he was gone she turned to me sharply. "Now listen, Pete, we need to get one more thing straight here. If you're going to be part of this, then Sammy is, too. He's a good kid. He looks up to you, and you need to be nice to him. So don't roll your eyes and reject all of his ideas just because he's younger than us. Who knows? He may just help us figure this thing out. Got it?"

"Okay," I replied. Just then, Sammy came running back in from the porch. I smiled at him and asked, "What did they say?"

"They said we could!"

"Great, let's go!" said Ali.

We put the cards away and made for the beach. Mom and Dad stopped us on the porch and made us put on fresh coats of sunscreen, and we were off. I thought about which way the attackers had run after the fight, and remembered that most of them took off when Ali's dad first called out. They had gone south, past Ali's house, so that's the direction we walked. The tide was still pretty high, so we had to walk in the dry, loose sand closest to the dunes. It made for a slow walk, but it also meant there was less beach to scan, so we forged on.

There is only the one jetty and a handful of houses between our house and the South End of Pawleys, but the beach stretches a long way after that before the creek finally meets the ocean. That southern expanse is a popular spot for day-trippers, fishermen, and seashell enthusiasts, and there's plenty of beach even at high tide. So, it's often the most crowded part of the island. Today was no exception. Families were walking, building sandcastles, and picnicking in the sand. Old men and young hopefuls were fishing in the creek, and of course the water was full of swimmers, boogie boarders, and a small boat a little farther out. We stopped for a minute to take in the scene, and I realized this might be a tougher mission than I had originally thought. But Ali wasn't fazed, and immediately asked Sammy and me, "So, does anyone look familiar?"

"Not yet, but let's walk around a little," I replied.

"Good answer, Pete," she said.

We continued walking. Small groups of people were peppered all across the beach, and I examined each of them carefully to see if they fit our profile. Most of them were families, although there were a few teenagers here and there. Ali recognized one of them as the girl Brian had met on their walk yesterday. She was sitting in a beach chair next to another girl, sunbathing. Ali pointed her out and we closed in quickly. When we were standing right next to her chair, Ali said, "Excuse me . . . Marcy, right? You met me and my brother yesterday. His name is Brian. Remember?"

Marcy quickly perked up and said, "Brian? Yeah, of course I remember. Cute guy. He said he would meet me down here today, but I haven't seen him. Where is he?"

Ali told her what happened. Marcy seemed genuinely upset, and when Ali finished the story, Marcy asked if there was anything she could do to help.

"Actually, we're trying to find out who did it. We think it was a group of three or four boys about your age. Any idea who it might have been?"

Marcy shook her head. "Sorry, but this is only my

second day here. I haven't really had time to meet a lot of people yet. But I'll definitely let you know if I hear anything. Tell Brian I hope he feels better soon!"

We kept searching the South End. No one stood out as the potential troublemakers. The sun was stifling hot, and I felt even more drained from focusing on our mission. I wanted to lighten the mood, so I tapped Sammy on the shoulder and said, "Tag, you're It!" and started running. Ali quickly followed me.

When we were a safe distance from my brother, she stopped and said, "I told you not to pick on him!"

"What do you mean?" I asked.

"He's so much younger, we'll have to slow up so he can catch us!"

"Oh no, we won't. He's the best Tag player I know. Just look, you'll see."

We both turned to locate Sammy, but he was nowhere to be found. "Where did he go?" Ali asked.

"This is how he plays Tag. It's like Hide-and-Seek, only he hides when *he's* It. Then he sneaks up on someone and tags them when they're least expecting it. It's a pretty good strategy, really."

"Yeah, it is, but where is he hiding? There's no good places out here on the beach."

"There's *tons* of good places out here, if you know

where to look," I said. "He could be walking behind someone, or ducking under an umbrella, or behind a sandcastle. He may have even gone in the water, even though Mom and Dad aren't here. You can look for him if you want to, but the best way to find him is to just ignore him and let him come out."

Ali giggled and started walking casually back toward our houses. I walked beside her, forgetting our quest and instead searching keenly for my brother. I spotted him digging in the sand near a few other kids, hiding perfectly in plain sight. I pointed him out to Ali, but she insisted we pretend not to see him. We started telling each other about our lives back home, and we walked right past Sammy without another glance in his direction.

Ali was from a small town in Tennessee. She was in the same grade as me in school, and in fact, our birthdays were only a week apart. Growing up with an older brother, she often had to act older than she actually was, which ended up giving her a very mature approach to things. When she told me her father was strict, I laughed and said there was no way he was worse than my dad. So, we started comparing stories. To my surprise, she was able to match me tale for tale, and we laughed and sympathized with each other as we walked under the hot afternoon sun. We could have kept talking all day, but a sudden buzzing sound in the water distracted me.

I looked out and stopped in my tracks. Ali stopped, too, and followed my stare out past the breakers.

Zipping in and out of the waves were three jet skis, driven by three boys with bright-blonde hair and matching blue swim trunks. I immediately recognized them as the kids from the bridge yesterday. Now they were yelling and jumping high off the waves, one after another. My smile faded and my jovial voice went soft and grim. "That's them."

Ali's tone changed instantly, as well. We were back on the case. "On the jet skis? Are you sure?"

"Pretty sure. They match everything I can remember seeing last night. And I saw the three of them yesterday afternoon, too, when we first got here. They were just sitting around doing nothing, like they were bored. Can you imagine? And today they go straight to riding jet skis. I bet they were walking on the beach last night, randomly met your brother, and had nothing better to do than jump him."

"Okay then," Ali said.

We stood there watching them for a few minutes. They were clearly having fun, and it made my blood boil to think they could do something so terrible last night, then laugh and play today like nothing happened. I'm sure Ali was feeling the same way, or even more so, since her brother was the victim. I said to her, "I hope they fall off those things."

As if on cue, one of them drove into a wave at a bad angle and was thrown off the back of the boat. The other two saw him and went to help him, but they turned toward each other and ended up colliding head-on. The jolt of the accident sent both boys flying. Ali and I looked at each other in pure astonishment, then burst out laughing.

We watched as all three of them swam back to their jet skis and struggled to climb back on. One of them slipped off so many times that the other two had to help him once they were back in their own seats. Their smiles and cheers long gone, they revved their engines loudly and motored off toward the north. We watched them as long as we could, hoping we would be lucky enough to see where they stopped. But they soon disappeared past a few jetties.

Ali said, "Well, we've made some great progress. Next time we'll have to walk that way and see if we can track them down. But I'm really hot right now. Let's just go home and get your parents to come out so we can go swimming."

"Sounds good," I replied.

We started walking back toward the house. Before long, we reached the jetty and carefully climbed over. As soon as we were safely standing on the other side, I saw a little hand appear out of nowhere and tap Ali on the arm.

"TAG! You're It!" Sammy said, and he scurried away down the beach.

CHAPTER 5

WE CHASED EACH OTHER HOME, PLAYING TAG the whole way. When we finally arrived we were sticky with sweat and blazing hot, so we went inside to get some water and rest for a few minutes. But before long we were ready to go swimming, so we talked Dad into coming down to the beach. To our surprise, he actually got in the water with us. He brought a ball and we played Keep Away, all of us diving and splashing and laughing for a solid hour. Then we saw Ali's dad standing on the beach, so Dad said it was time to go in.

We were fully exhausted again when we dragged

ourselves onto the sand. Our dads talked for a minute, and we learned that Brian was feeling a little better. Mr. Baxter then asked his daughter, "So, how was your day?"

"Dad, it was great! We played and ate lunch and went for a walk and everything. Pete and Sammy really cheered me up. Can I please hang out with them again tomorrow?"

"Well, sure," her dad said. Then he looked at me. "You really know how to treat a lady if *this* one's impressed. She doesn't have too many friends back home."

"Well, the kids in Tennessee are missing out, sir," I replied. "We had a lot of fun today, too. Thanks for letting her play!" My eyes met Ali's and she gave me the most endearing look I had ever seen. "See you tomorrow," I told her.

"Bye, Pete," she said sincerely. Then her voice was instantly cheery again. "And bye, Sammy! Y'all have a good evening!"

We went inside, took showers, and got fully dressed for the first time all day. By then dinner was ready: pimento-cheese burgers. It's funny, neither Sammy nor I normally like pimento cheese, but those burgers are awesome. Mom asked us about our day, and Sammy and I told her what we could without mentioning our hunt for the older kids. After dinner we played a few rounds of UNO, and then it was bedtime. Sammy jumped into bed and embraced

Alfonso like a long-lost friend. My sleep was deep and peaceful, with no interruptions.

The next day was Tuesday. Sammy and I got up, ate breakfast, and made for the beach straight away. Mom and Dad came down with us and set up their chairs in the usual spot. It was low tide, so there was lots of room to play, and Sammy and I took full advantage. We ran around and drew pictures by dragging our toes through the damp sand. We splashed in the calm water and searched for Pawleys Shells. At one point Sammy said, "Pete, why do you keep staring at Ali's house?"

"I'm not staring at her house!" I said defensively.

"Yes, you are! You've looked up there, like, a hundred times since we've been out here."

"No, I haven't!" I said, and I gave him a little shove. He pushed back, so I pushed him harder and he fell backward into the water. It was shallow and barely covered his legs as he sat there, stunned. He wasn't hurt, but I reached down to help him up anyway.

As Sammy got back to his feet, I heard heavy footsteps behind me. I turned to see Dad towering over me. His eyes were covered by sunglasses, but I knew exactly what they looked like: thin, piercing, angry.

"What was that about?" he asked harshly.

"Nothing, I'm sorry. I didn't mean to push him so hard," I said calmly.

"What do you mean, you didn't mean to push him so hard? He's half your size. What did you think was going to happen? And why were you pushing in the first place?"

"No reason. I mean, it's stupid."

"I'm listening," he said firmly.

"Well, um, he was . . . making fun of me."

"Are you serious?" Dad yelled, "*That's* why you pushed him? Listen to me, son. He's your little brother. He's going to be making fun of you for the rest of your life. It's just what little brothers do. But as the *big* brother, it's *your* responsibility to keep yourself under control and not let it bother you. You could really hurt him without even trying. Now, tell him you're sorry!"

I apologized to Sammy. Dad finished by saying, "Now, we've had a great start to the week. Let's not ruin it by fighting over things that don't matter, okay?"

"Yes, sir."

"Good, thank you." His face and voice both softened. "Now, I bet if you go knock on Ali's door, she'd probably come out and play with y'all."

I was mortified. Had I really been staring at her house so much that both Sammy *and* Dad had noticed? I mean, I did want her to come out, both to play and to continue our quest. But it had never even occurred to me to just go knock on her door. With Sammy on my heels, I walked to her house and up the front stairs.

Her mom answered the door. "Well, hello there, boys! How are you today?"

"Just fine, ma'am, thank you," I said. "Can Ali come out and play?"

"Well, sure!" She leaned her head back inside the door and called, "Ali! Peter and Sammy want to play!"

From somewhere inside I heard Ali respond, "Be right there! I just need to get my bathing suit on!" Footsteps ran from one room to another, and a door closed.

Mrs. Baxter said, "I'm so glad you came over. Ali has talked about nothing but you two ever since she got home yesterday."

I could feel my cheeks turning red, so I changed the subject. "How is Brian today?"

"Oh, you're so sweet to ask. He's doing much better. One more day inside and he'll be ready to enjoy some fun on the beach tomorrow."

"Then we can all play together!" Sammy said.

She smiled at him and said, "I'm sure he would love that."

Just then Ali came dashing out the door. She breezed right past her mom, tapped Sammy and me on our shoulders, and said, "Okay boys, let's go!"

But her mom stopped her. "Just a minute, young lady! You need sunscreen." As she sprayed the lotion, she added, "If you talk to Peter's parents, remember your sir's and ma'am's. And if they feed you again, you'd better say thank you."

"Yes, ma'am," said Ali, annoyed. When her mom was finished, we said goodbye and headed for the beach. But halfway down the stairs, Ali stopped and turned back toward the house. "Oh, and Mom!" she called. Her mom raised her eyebrows. Ali said, "His name is PETE!"

Our new friend needed no cheering up today. She was happy and carefree on the beach, her curly red hair blowing gently in the breeze and her laugh contagious even to the random people walking by. We swam and played Tag, and then Mom and Dad got up from their chairs to help us build sandcastles.

As the morning wore on, the tide rose, and before long the waves were approaching Mom and Dad's chairs. They took that as a cue for lunchtime. Despite our protests, they made us go inside to eat, so we devoured some sandwiches and asked if we could go back outside.

"Well, I need a longer break," Dad said. "So, I'm staying here, which you know means no swimming. And it's high tide, so there's not much beach. What are you guys going to do out there?"

"Nothing! I mean, maybe we'll just take a little walk? We can go north this time and see if there are any Pawleys Shells," I said.

"Okay, well just put on some more sunscreen and be careful."

"Yes, sir," I replied, and all three of us coated our skin with a fresh layer of lotion. As we walked out, Ali made sure to thank my parents for lunch. Then we were on our way, eyes squinting in the bright midday sun, yet as keen as wolves hunting prey.

Chapter 6

WE DIDN'T SAY MUCH AS WE EXPLORED the beach. Our stomachs were full and the sand was soft, so we walked pretty slowly. But some clouds had rolled in off the ocean while we were inside, so at least there was some shade. The tide had peaked a little earlier today and was already waning. I remembered this was normal; the cycle adjusts ever so slightly every day, and by the end of the week the timing of the tides would have completely reversed itself.

We had walked three whole jetties, about thirty houses from ours, before we started losing hope. The beach was sparsely populated, and the people we did see were of no use to our case. Sammy had picked up so many seashells that the pockets of his swim trunks were overflowing. I told him he should put some back or else his pants might fall down. Ali thought that was funny. Sammy did not.

"Let's just check one more jetty," Ali suggested, so we kept walking. We climbed over the rocks and examined the beach on the other side. "Nothing. I guess we should head back home," she said.

But there *was* something. Ali just didn't realize it because she's never been here before. On the beach only a few houses up, an empty flatbed trailer was resting in the sand.

"Wait!" I said, and my brother and Ali paused. "That's a jet-ski trailer."

The implication was obvious, but Sammy said, "Then that's probably the bad guys' house!"

"It could be," I answered, "but we can't tell for sure. We need to come back later and see if it's the same jet skis from yesterday."

Ali was not so easily deterred. "But Pete, this was a long walk, and we're already here now. Why don't we just wait and see if they come back sometime soon?"

So we climbed down off the jetty and waited. Sammy picked up even more shells while Ali and I dipped our feet in the water. We kept our distance, but watched closely for any sign of activity around the trailer. Time dragged slowly, and soon Sammy wanted to go home. We were discussing how much longer to wait when we heard the motors out in the water.

Approaching quickly from the north were three jet skis. I instantly recognized them as the same ones from before, driven by the same three boys with bright-blonde hair and today, matching yellow swim trunks. We stayed near the jetty and watched as they approached the shore but stopped short of the sand. Then, two of them jumped off their boats and ran up to grab the trailer and drag it into the water. They took turns driving the watercraft straight onto the flatbed, then all three struggled together to pull it back onto the beach and up to the dunes, where the tide wouldn't reach. They talked for a minute, and I thought they were going to go inside, but then in a flash, they ran back out into the waves.

"Let's go," said Ali, but instead of walking toward them she waded deeper into the water.

"What are you doing? We're not allowed to go swimming without our parents watching!" Sammy cried.

Ali replied calmly, "It's okay, Sammy, we're not going in too far. Only up to our knees, maybe. I just want to be casual when we first meet them so they don't get too defensive right away. They're older than us, and we just want to ask them some questions for now. Once they admit what they did to Brian, we can lower the hammer."

Sammy eyed me for approval and I nodded, so he entered the water. Ali started splashing us, so we splashed back, and when we did she turned and started running away from us—straight toward the blonde boys. I caught on and started chasing after her, splashing and laughing. Sammy followed along, too. Soon Ali was really close to one of the older boys, and she turned toward us and started running backward until she bumped right into him.

"Oh! Sorry!" she said to him.

Surprisingly, the boy smiled at her, and in a slow, thick Southern accent he said, "No problem." Then he nodded toward Sammy and me and added, "Want me to help you fend off them boys?"

Ali was clearly taken aback by his friendliness, but she was quick to answer, "Oh, no thanks. They're my friends. We're just playing."

"A'right," the boy said. He started back toward his blonde companions, but Ali started splashing wildly in all directions, clearly intending to get him involved in our splash warfare. It worked. He was catching spray from Ali's crazy episode, so he began splashing back in retaliation. And he was good. He let loose long, deep strokes from underwater that drenched all three of us in a shower of salt water. The other two boys took notice and joined in, as well, all three of them using the same highly refined and highly effective motion. Sammy and I hurried to reinforce Ali, but the blonde boys were just too much for us.

"Truce!" I yelled out, and all of the splashing stopped. When the water settled I got my first good, close look at the boys' faces, and it became very clear why they all used the same exact splashing method. It also made sense why they were always wearing matching swim trunks.

They were triplets.

"Y'all okay?" the first boy asked us.

"Yeah, we're fine," said Ali. Then, ever so slyly, she lectured, "But you guys shouldn't be picking on people you randomly meet on the beach."

"We didn't mean nothin', we just splash away and don't know how to back off once we get goin'. I'm real sorry. My name's Tim, and these are my brothers, Tom and Davy Ray."

His politeness put Ali in a quandary. She really didn't want to give these boys our names yet, but her Southern manners got the best of her and she knew she had to respond in kind. "I'm Ali, and these are my friends Pete and Sammy. It's nice to meet y'all."

"Nice to meet y'all, too," Tim said, and he reached out

his hand to shake ours. His brothers followed his lead, and we were all properly met. Then Tim asked, "When did y'all get to Pawleys? We've been here since Sunday morning, but I don't remember seein' y'all yet."

Ali continued the conversation. "We've been here since Sunday, too. I'm pretty sure we saw you on your jet skis yesterday. Down by the South End of the island?"

Tim nodded. "Yep, we were down there yesterday. Fun ride. Y'all might be a little young to drive 'em yourselves, but if you want to ride on the back with us, that'd probably be okay. Whadaya say?"

I could tell Ali was growing impatient. We hadn't walked all this way to make new friends. It was time to go in for the kill. "Maybe some other time. But I think Pete here might've seen you on the beach Sunday night, too. Would y'all have been out for a late walk or something?"

The brothers' faces turned stone cold. Their eyes widened and they exchanged knowing looks with each other. Clearly, we had found the right boys.

Ali pressed them. "Come on, guys, we know everything. Just tell us what happened and we might not get you in too much trouble."

"Trouble?" Tom said, "Why would we get in trouble?"

Although Ali was handling things perfectly, I couldn't help but interject. "What do you mean? Of *course* you're in trouble! You can't just beat up some stranger and get away with no consequences! I saw everything! You jumped him and didn't stop until his dad came out and almost busted you right then and there. And what did he do to deserve it? Huh? Come on, tell us why you beat up Ali's brother!"

The blonde boys looked even more shocked now. "Your *brother*?" Tim said, and behind him Davy Ray buried his face in his hands.

"Yes, my brother," Ali replied simply.

"And you think *we* beat him up?" Tim asked.

"I saw you do it," I answered.

Tim took a deep breath and remained calm. "Look, I know we just met, so I don't want to go accusing anyone of seein' things wrong, but we didn't beat anybody up that night. If you really saw what happened, then you should know we were trying to help that guy."

Now it was our turn to be shocked. "*Help* him?" Ali said. She looked at me abruptly and asked, "Pete, is this possible? You said it was dark and you couldn't see much. Could it have been someone else that attacked Brian, while these guys defended him?"

I thought back. In the melee of that night, I guess I really couldn't distinguish any one participant's role versus the others, or even tell exactly how many people were involved, for that matter. But someone definitely beat Brian up; he had the bruises to prove it. So, was it possible that someone else was the offender, and that these triplets were really just nice guys that tried to help a stranger in a fight?

"I guess . . . I guess it's possible," I said.

Ali looked back at Tim. "Okay then, if you were trying to help, then you must have gotten a good look at the guy that actually did it. Do you know him?"

Again, the triplets' faces went white. They looked frightened. Tim swallowed hard and said slowly, "I guess you could say we know *of* him . . . "

Ali pressed again. "What's that supposed to mean? Who was it?"

Tim's eyes were now aghast and his hands were shaking. Tom and Davy Ray were silent but clearly terrified at the memory, as well. At length Tim answered, his lips trembling: "*It was the Gray Man!*"

Chapter 7

"*IMPOSSIBLE!*" I SHOUTED, AND MY BLOOD WAS instantly boiling at the accusation. I could tell Sammy was upset, too. I heard him gasp and then splash around in the water. Ali obviously didn't know why my brother and I were upset, and the triplets were surprised by our reactions, as well. But I would have to explain later. At that moment, I just needed to hear Tim change his story. "Seriously man, that's not funny. Tell us who it really was!"

Tim's face was still pale and his expression didn't change. "I know it ain't funny, that's why I ain't laughin'. We were walkin' along and ran into your brother. Since he's our age, we started talkin' and gettin' along real good. Your brother's a nice guy, for sure. But then we saw . . . *him* . . . just running down the beach from out of nowhere. He spotted the four of us and walked right up and pushed your brother to the ground, just out of the blue like that. Tom here yelled at him and tried to grab the guy, but he ducked out of our reach. Once your brother got up, he yelled, too, sayin' it was a cheap shot and to come back and fight like a man. That set him off, and he ran at your brother with his fist cocked back. I didn't know what to do. I didn't think I should fight with the Gray Man, but your brother hadn't done nothin' wrong. So, I took a swing at him as he ran toward us. He dodged me and then stopped right in front of our group. 'Come on now, we really don't wanna fight,' I told him, and for a second it looked like he was thinking better of gettin' into it four against one.

"But then, without sayin' a word, he just hauled off and hit your brother right in the face. He followed your brother to the ground and just kep' hittin' him, and we all three jumped in to try to pull them two apart. But he was strong as an ox and fully committed, and even working together it was tough to move him. Then your dad called down from the house, and we didn't want to deal with no parents, so we split. We didn't even pay attention to which direction we ran. Turns out, we went the wrong way and had to circle back a few minutes later. But by then everybody else was gone, and all we saw when we walked by was some scuffed-up sand. I wouldn't have believed it either if I hadn't seen it with my own eyes, but that's the honest truth of what happened."

I stood there knee-deep in the ocean and listened closely to Tim, trying my hardest to remember what I saw that night and find any possible flaws in his story. But as best I could recall, his account of the fight perfectly fit how I saw it. Even Sammy was nodding along as he spoke, further confirming that we all shared the same understanding of what happened. There was just one problem.

"Okay," I said, "maybe I believe you. It does sound a lot like what I saw and heard that night. But I'm telling you, there is *just no way* the Gray Man beat anybody up! It had to be someone else!"

Sammy backed me up. "Yeah! He's a good ghost. He would never hurt anybody!"

"Wait, *ghost*?" Ali exclaimed, and I remembered that she was new here and had no idea what we were talking about. "The Gray Man is a *ghost*?"

"Yeah," I told her, "and Sammy's right, he's a good ghost. That's why it had to be somebody else." I looked at Tim. "You know, like, a *real person*?"

Davy Ray finally piped up and said, "Oh, it was a real person all right. He musta' come back to life or somethin'. But we've been comin' to Pawleys for ten years, and we know the Gray Man when we seen him!"

His brothers nodded in agreement, all of them still a little shaken but now reanimated in defense of their story. Ali couldn't stand to be in the dark any longer. "All right, all right, let's just all take a few deep breaths and back up for a minute. Can someone please tell me who the Gray Man is?"

"Yes," I said, "but let's go sit in the sand."

So, all six of us strode out of the shallow water and sat in a circle on the beach. It was pretty hot despite the shade from the clouds, and we had been on our feet all afternoon. I knew we had a long walk back to the house coming up, so I thought a little rest was in order. Besides, what better way to tell a ghost story than sitting around campfire-style? When we were all settled I began the tale, just like Dad always told it to me.

"The Gray Man was once a young soldier who lived on Pawleys Island. He was strong, kind, and well-loved in the small community. One day he met a beautiful young lady named Alice, and soon they were deeply in love. The soldier went to Alice's father to ask for her hand in marriage, but her father strictly forbade it. In fact, that very night he packed up the family and took to the sea so the two could never be together. The soldier slipped into a deep depression. He started spending long days just walking the beach, staring out into the ocean, watching for her ship to return. But she was gone too long, and eventually the young man died of heartbreak.

"Of course, Alice never forgot her suitor, and as soon as she could, she *did* come back to Pawleys. Upon learning of her soldier's death, she, too, became depressed and took to walking on the beach. She was walking one dark and windy night when she saw a tall, shadowy, gray figure walking toward her in the sand. She immediately recognized him as her long-lost love, but this was no happy reunion. His only words were a warning to leave the island at once. . . . Then, he disappeared!

"Without thinking twice, Alice ran home and packed her things, then rushed to the mainland and got as far away as she could. That same night, a hurricane struck Pawleys. Much of the island was destroyed, but Alice's house and family were spared. When she heard this news, Alice had no doubt that her love had saved her, and the legend was born. To this day, the Gray Man still roams the beach before bad storms, and seeing him is both a warning and a sign of good luck—you know there is a terrible storm coming, but you and your house will be safe.

"There are stories of people seeing him all the way back before hurricanes had names, and each time the person's house was spared from the storm. Not too long ago, a resident saw the Gray Man and fled the approaching hurricane. When they returned to check out the damage, they found the house next door was completely demolished. But, not only was their house still standing, they realized they had accidentally left some beach towels hanging to dry on the front porch . . . and they were still there!

"But there is one last piece to the story. After seeing her love and fleeing the island, Alice was never quite the same. She died soon after, but her body was returned to Pawleys to be buried in her hometown. It is said that her spirit still yearns to marry her sweet soldier, and to wear a wedding ring that symbolizes their love. So if any married woman visits Alice's grave, she had better hold onto her ring tightly, or Alice just might steal it!"

When I finished the story, our group sat in silence for several minutes. Ali was the first to speak. "Well, I must say, that certainly does not sound like the kind of ghost that would attack someone for no reason—or any reason, for that matter. Is there another Gray Man that's, like, this one's evil twin?"

She was being sarcastic, but the triplets took her seriously and shook their heads in unison. Tim said, "Nope. We couldn't believe it ourselves after it happened. We came home and asked our parents if they had ever heard of the Gray Man hurtin' anybody, and they said no. But like I said, we know the story, just like Pete here told it. There's just nobody else it could have been."

"What did he look like, exactly?" Ali asked.

Tom gave the description. "He was tall, dressed in all gray, of course, like an ol'-timey soldier, but with a cape and a wide hat so we couldn't see his face. He moved real fast, and when he walked it looked like his feet just barely touched the ground, almost like he was . . . floating. But when we grabbed him, he felt solid, not like those ghosts on TV that can walk through walls and stuff. That's about all I could see."

We sat still for another moment. Then, decidedly, Ali said, "Well, I guess we'll just have to find him." She tapped Sammy and me on the shoulders. "Come on, guys. We should probably head home." She stood up and said to the blonde boys, "It was nice meeting y'all. Thanks for your help. Maybe we'll see you around." She turned and started walking quickly toward the jetty.

Sammy and I stood up and rushed to shake hands with the triplets. Tim said, "I'm sorry about all the confusion.

And I'm sorry you two had to see that happen the other night. It's just a strange situation for all of us, I guess. Tell her brother we hope he's okay. And I meant it about the jet skis—y'all just come on back if you want to ride 'em."

"Thanks," I said, and then Sammy and I ran to catch up with Ali.

She was already halfway over the jetty when my brother and I reached the base of the rocks. I thought it was weird that she had walked off so abruptly, and she didn't even stop to wait for us when I shouted her name from a short distance back. I climbed as fast as I could and caught up to her by the time she jumped down the other side. She kept walking, but I gently grabbed her arm and asked, "Hey, are you okay?"

She gave me the saddest, most heart-wrenching look I had ever seen, then fell to her knees and started to cry.

CHAPTER 8

"WHAT'S THE MATTER?" I ASKED HER. AND I truly didn't know. Over the last day and a half I had watched this girl tough it out through what had to be one of the hardest things she's ever gone through. She was a little quiet yesterday morning, but only in front of our parents. As soon as we started talking about Brian, she was intelligent, observant, and decisive. And while we seemed to have hit a bit of a snag in our investigation just now, we had made a ton of progress in a short amount of time. I sat down next to her in the sand with my hand still on her arm. Sammy joined us, also concerned for our friend.

"Oh Pete," she said finally, "what are we supposed to do now? We can't go chasing ghosts!"

"Sure we can, you said it yourself!"

"But I didn't mean it. That was just for show. I didn't want those boys to see how upset I was. They're convinced it was the Gray Man, and no offense, but you didn't see enough to prove otherwise. But then you told that story, and now I know why you think it couldn't have been him. So we're stuck, don't you see? Those three boys were our best chance to find the bad guy, and they told us it was a ghost who saves people from hurricanes!"

"It's okay, just take a deep breath. For what it's worth, I still don't believe it was the Gray Man. I *won't* believe it. I love this island and everything about it. This place lives in every fiber of my being, and that story lives at the very heart of Pawleys. To say the Gray Man hurt someone is like taking away the foundation of everything I hold sacred—all the traditions, games, family time, even the same old stupid meals Dad makes every year. And if that happens, well, I might as well just stay home next summer. And I *definitely* don't want to do that. So now we just have even more reason to get to the bottom of this. There *has* to be some explanation, and we're going to find it!"

Ali looked at me and smiled. Through her tear-soaked eyes I felt a warmth I had never felt before. She wrapped her arms around me and hugged me tight, and my heart raced. I hugged her back.

Sammy interrupted our embrace by sticking his head between ours and throwing his arms wildly around us both as best he could. Ali and I laughed and let him join in. "I hate to break up the love fest here, but we should get going," he said. Ali took a deep breath to mark the official end of her crying, and we stood up and started walking home.

It wasn't long before we saw my parents walking toward us. Sammy ran ahead to meet them and jumped into Mom's arms. But even from a distance, I could tell Dad was angry. We had been gone a long time, and walked much farther than we should have. All I could hope was that he wouldn't yell at me in front of Ali.

He didn't yell, but when we reached them I knew I was going to get grilled. I could see in his eyes he was truly furious. He skipped over any manner of cordial greeting and made his position known: "Peter, I trusted you to be responsible down here on the beach without us. I knew you were going for a walk, but do you have any idea how long you've been gone?"

I tried to use my most innocent-sounding voice. "An hour?"

"Try three hours."

"Really?"

"Yes, son, really."

"Oh. I'm sorry, I—"

But Ali cut me off. "It was my fault, Mr. Prince. I've never been to Pawleys before, and I told Pete I wanted to walk all the way to the North End. I guess I didn't realize how far it was."

Dad's face hardened even more. "You went all the way to the *North End*?!"

"No, sir!" Ali hurried to continue on my behalf. "We only got a few jetties up the beach and then we made some new friends. So, we stayed and played with them in front of their house for a while. Their parents were outside with us the whole time."

Her lie was so seamlessly woven into her speech that even I believed her for a moment. Dad raised one eyebrow and turned to my brother. This was his usual way of trying to catch me in a lie, because Sammy doesn't mind getting me in trouble. He'll call me out in front of Dad every time. "Sammy, did you make some new friends?"

"Yes, sir," he said.

"And their house is close by here?"

"Yes, sir."

"And their parents were watching you *the whole time*?"

"Yes, sir."

Dad shot one more glare at me and held it for what seemed like forever. I simply smiled in return. Eventually his face softened and he said, "Well, you still should have been aware of how long you were gone, Peter. I can't give you new privileges if you can't be responsible with them."

"Yes, sir. I'm sorry, Dad."

"Okay. Well, let's get home. The tide's going out. I was thinking we could float the creek."

Sammy and I both jumped. "Yeah!" we shouted at the same time. I said to Ali, "You're going to love this." It had been a long and emotional day already, and floating the creek sounded like the perfect way to relax the rest of the afternoon away.

The creek that makes Pawleys an island is tidal, so the water is constantly flowing like a river in one direction or the other. Many houses have a small dock that extends out into the water with a sitting area at the end. They're perfect for crabbing, shooting bottle rockets, and hanging out. And they're perfect for launching rafts. When the tide is going out, you can jump onto a raft from your crab dock and float to the South End. The long stretch of beach there makes it easy to know when to get out, and it gives you a nice, big target that's nearly impossible to overshoot. So, there's no real danger of drifting out to sea. Floating the creek has been a family tradition for as long as I can remember, and will continue to be for as long as I have anything to say about it.

Mom and Dad had already blown up four rafts, and they helped us carry them across the street and onto our crab dock. "Here you go, Alison. Have fun," Dad said, and he handed her a raft.

"But wait," she said. "There are five of us. Are you and Sammy going to share?"

"Nope, everybody gets their own raft. I'm the driver."

Ali didn't understand, but I told her not to worry about it. She shrugged and followed me to the edge of the dock. Then Mom, Sammy, Ali, and I carefully descended into the creek. We grabbed hold of each others' rafts to stay together, waved goodbye to Dad, and let the relaxation begin.

I say it's relaxing, but it's not really. We were only stationary on our rafts for a few moments before my brother slipped off of his—on purpose. He swam underwater toward me and pushed up underneath my raft, flipping me over into the water. Sammy laughed jovially, but Ali caught on and dunked him while his attention was still on me. Mom joined in, moving her foot stealthily under the rafts to pull Ali's out from under her. We each climbed back onto our rafts, but as soon as we did, someone was right there to get us wet again. This went on almost the whole way down the creek, until near the end when we were all exhausted from swimming and laughing. We finally settled down just in time to paddle toward the bank and pull ourselves and our gear onto the sand.

To Ali's surprise (but no one else's), Dad was standing on the beach waiting for us. As we dragged our rafts toward him, the car came into view and Ali connected the dots. "You're going to drive us home so we don't have to walk, right?"

"Right." Dad smiled.

The car was in a small parking lot where the main road ends. The sun was starting to go down, so there were a few other people loading up their beach stuff to go home. I didn't pay much attention to them as I tossed my raft in the trunk. But as I approached the car door, I overheard something that made me stop in my tracks.

" . . . the Gray Man . . . "

I darted my eyes down the row of cars and saw a kid, about my age, sitting on the tailgate of a black pickup truck. He was crying and pleading with his parents, but they were shaking their heads. Before I could make out anything else they were saying, they got into the truck and drove off.

I looked at Ali. She and Sammy were both watching the truck as it rolled away.

CHAPTER 9

WE COULDN'T TALK ABOUT THIS NEW DEVELOPment with Mom and Dad in the front seat, but all three of us were definitely thinking it. The Gray Man had struck again! What did this mean? I still refused to believe it was him, but then why had four people now accused him of wrongdoing? Tim, Tom, and Davy Ray were Pawleys Island regulars, and this new kid at least knew enough to identify the local legend. I couldn't make any sense of it. But one thing was clear: tomorrow we were going back to the South End. Brian was attacked in the middle of the night, but right now it was just getting dark. There had to be some additional witnesses this time.

Ali's dad was waiting in our driveway when we got home. As a very pleasant surprise, Brian was with him! Ali ran over to greet her brother with a big hug. He cringed, still not fully healed, but hugged her back. Even though the daylight was fading, I could tell his face was still badly bruised, and a few bandages hid even worse injuries. He was doing his best to stand up straight, but it looked like one of his legs hurt, too.

"Brian! I'm so glad to see you out of the house!" Ali cried. "I'd like you to officially meet my new friends. This is Pete, his brother, Sammy, and their parents, Mr. and Mrs. Prince."

Brian shook all our hands and said, "I feel like I know you already from how much Ali's been talking about you. Thanks for keeping her busy while I've been holed up inside."

"It's been our pleasure," Dad said. "We're just glad you're feeling better."

Then Ali started rehashing all of the things we had done that day—leaving out the more exciting details, of course—while our parents stood off to the side and started chatting.

Since I had been there for everything Ali was talking about, I tried to listen in on the grown-up conversation. It turned out to be very interesting. Mom commented on how good Brian looked, but Dad cut right to the chase. "I still don't understand why you haven't called the police. This was assault. Whoever did it belongs in jail!"

"I know," Ali's dad replied, "but Brian can't even describe the guy. It was pitch black, and he was wearing a hat that covered his face. Why file a police report that gives the cops no chance of catching the offender? And even if they did arrest somebody, any decent defense attorney could get the case thrown out for lack of evidence. Look, at this point I'm just glad he's okay, and I'm *very* glad those other boys were there to help him. Otherwise . . . well, I don't want to think about what could've happened if he was alone."

It took me a minute, but this made sense when I thought about it from Mr. Baxter's perspective. Ali was the only one in their family that knew the story of the Gray Man, and she only learned it a few hours ago. To Brian, there was nothing unusual about the way his attacker was dressed, and if the gray hat was covering his face, then Brian couldn't have seen any distinguishing features or even guess his age. Even if I told the cops what I saw and everything we had found so far, they would probably laugh us out of the police station when we told them the prime suspect was the Gray Man. So, as much as I would love to have the cops chasing this guy, we were on our own.

Both conversations ended and we all said goodnight. Ali hugged me. I was expecting her to be sincere like she was yesterday when we parted, but instead she whispered, "Big day tomorrow. Let's start early." I nodded, and then she smiled and went back to her house with her dad and brother.

The four of us went inside and had dinner: barbecue pork, Brunswick stew, and coleslaw. Dad said this was an especially important tradition, because it was a tribute to the pig pickin's they used to have at Pawleys when he was a kid. I've never been to a pig pickin', but I like barbecue, so whatever it's a tribute to is fine with me.

After dinner it was time for bed. Mom wanted Sammy and me to take showers, but Dad said we were just going to get dirty again tomorrow, so what's the point? Mom rolled her eyes and sent us to our room with a kiss. Sammy and I smiled at each other. No showers? Talk about a new privilege! We did, at least, put on some clean pajamas over our sticky, salty skin. Then we climbed into bed, Sammy snuggled in with Alfonso, and my entire body melted into sleep.

That night I had a dream about the Gray Man. I was walking on the beach in the dark, and from out of nowhere he appeared and started running toward me. I froze, terrified. When he was just inches away, I saw his face, and there was a terror in his eyes unlike anything I had ever seen. I braced myself for an attack, but he flew right by me.

I spun around to see where he was going and found Ali and Brian just a few steps away. The Gray Man's gaze was locked on Brian, but Ali stood in front of her brother, her fists clenched at her sides and her chest proud. "I won't let you hurt him again!" she shouted.

But the ghost passed her, too, and started thrashing Brian, following him to the ground and beating him relentlessly. Ali started pounding on the Gray Man's back, trying to pull him off, but it did no good. She shouted frantically to me, "What are you doing, Pete? Come on!"

I ran toward my friends and cocked my arm to hit the specter. But just before I swung my fist, something in the sand caught my eye. I bent down and picked up an absolutely perfect Pawleys Island Shell. I have no idea why, but I held it up in front of the Gray Man's face.

He looked up at the shell and froze. The dread in his eyes vanished, and he suddenly looked old and tired. He stood up and lowered the brim of his hat so his face was hidden from view, but I could still feel his eyes staring into mine. Then he spoke.

"*Thank you, child. You understand the true spirit of this island, and you believe in me more than anyone has in a long time. Your heart is strong.*"

He started walking away, but I shouted after him, "Hey! Why have you been hurting people?"

Without stopping he replied, "*You already know the answer.*" Then he disappeared.

I woke up to a knock at the front door. The sun was shining brightly through the window, and I could smell coffee, so I knew at least one of my parents was already up. I heard footsteps move from the kitchen to the front door, then the door opened and Mom said, "Well, good morning, Ali! Come on in. I assume you're looking for the boys?"

"Yes, ma'am. I was hoping they could walk to the South End with me to look for Pawleys Shells. I'd really like to find one!"

"Well, I can't blame you. They're beautiful. But you have to be patient: they're very rare. Why don't you have a seat and I'll go get Peter and Sammy."

I leapt out of bed, horrified. It felt early, but no matter what time it was, I couldn't let Ali know I was still in bed. Sammy grumbled and slowly opened his eyes as I ditched my pajamas and struggled to throw on my swim trunks.

"Sammy, wake up!" I whispered loudly. "Ali's here, and we're going for a walk!"

As soon as he processed my words, he jumped up, too,

and changed clothes quickly. We snuck to the bathroom together and each squeezed a small drop of toothpaste onto our fingers, then rubbed it inside our mouths. This way it would smell like we had brushed our teeth without us actually having to. I also used some of Dad's deodorant, but Sammy wasn't interested in that. Mom was at our door when we opened it and casually entered the family room. I smiled at her and then greeted our guest.

"Oh hi, Ali! I thought I heard someone come in. Sammy and I were just playing in our room. What's up?"

"Good morning, Pete! I was wondering if you two wanted to go hunting for Pawleys Shells again? I was thinking we could go back to the South End."

Mom gave us a nod of approval, and as we rushed to put on sunscreen she asked if we wanted any breakfast. Sammy and I each grabbed a biscuit and took off, leaving a trail of crumbs through the living room as we ate and ran.

Chapter 10

THE TIDE WAS ALREADY COMING IN WHEN we began our Wednesday morning walk, and it reminded me that by the end of the week it would be full high tide at this time of morning, and then again in the evening. The sun was already bearing down on the beach, and with no wind at all, I knew this was going to be a very hot day. We were sweating before we even reached the first jetty.

We got to the top of the rocks and surveyed the South End. It was surprisingly crowded for this time of morning, which meant there was a decent chance some of the same people were here yesterday when the Gray Man struck. We climbed down and started examining the people in the crowd more closely, trying to pick out the right ones to approach with our questions. There were several families with younger kids; obviously we weren't going to talk to them. We didn't want to scare the little ones, and the fewer grown-ups involved, the better. There were some old men fishing and a few joggers. Some teenagers had set up a volleyball net, some chairs, and a small stereo. This group looked promising, especially after we recognized Marcy from our first trip down here the day after Brian was attacked. She was playing volleyball, so we kept our distance and didn't interrupt her. We looked around for other kids we could talk to, but it appeared Marcy was again our best chance for a clue.

When her game ended, we casually walked toward the group. We were just about to say hello when all three of us recognized someone else in the group. We hadn't noticed him because he was sitting in a chair watching, but when he saw us he got up and met us a little way out from the group.

"Hey, shrimp, what are you doing here?" Brian asked his sister.

"We're just looking for Pawleys Island Shells. And don't call me a shrimp!"

"Pawleys Island Shells, huh? All right, whatever you say. Look, please just don't embarrass me in front of these other kids. There are shells all over this island. Go look somewhere else, okay?"

Ali's voice turned high pitched, whiney, and noticeably louder. "But Brian, we wanted you to come with us!"

"Shut up! I just told you not to embarrass me! Now shoo!"

I could tell Ali was getting mad. She wasn't about to let Brian, of all people, interfere with our mission. I decided I should speak up and make sure the argument didn't get worse.

"Brian, we're not trying to embarrass you. We just have a quick question for Marcy and maybe a couple of the others here. I'll tell you what. How about you go ask Marcy to come over here? That way we won't even have to get any closer to the group. And as soon as she gets here, you can leave. Okay?"

Brian rolled his eyes but agreed. As he was jogging back to get Marcy, Ali said, "Pete, that was brilliant! We don't want Brian to hear what we're up to, so getting Marcy to come to us and then having Brian leave is absolutely perfect."

"Um, yeah, I guess so. But I didn't even think of it that way, I was just trying to get us a chance to talk to her."

"That's one of my favorite things about you, Pete. You're awesome without even trying to be."

This caught me off guard. This girl was complimenting

me again for doing nothing except being me. I didn't know what to say, but Marcy was approaching us so I managed to eke out, "You're awesome, too." Ali smiled, and then Marcy was standing in front of us.

"Hey, you three. What's up?"

"Hi, Marcy," Ali began. "We just wanted to ask you something. Were you down here on the beach yesterday? Around sunset?"

"Yeah, after dinner a group of us came down for a swim. We left when it got dark. Why?"

Ali eased into the questions. "Did you see anything . . . bad happen?"

"No, why? What happened?"

"Maybe nothing. We don't really know. There was a kid crying back by the creek and . . . we're trying to help him out." It was an odd choice of words for Ali, because we hadn't even met that kid. It would be a hard story to back up if Marcy or anyone else asked us for details. But we were lucky for now.

"Hmm. Well, I'm sorry I can't help. You guys just love looking for bad guys, don't you?"

I remembered that we had flat-out told her that we were trying to find out who beat Brian up when we first met her.

"Yeah, well, we haven't had much luck in that department. Thanks anyway," Ali said.

Before she walked off, I jumped in and asked, "Hey, one more thing. Did you see anyone dressed funny? Like, all gray clothes and a hat?"

"Ugh, what a weirdo. He just stood in the dunes watching us but never said anything. A couple of the guys wanted to go mess with him after we swam, but he was gone by then."

Ali retook the lead. "Wow, he does sound weird. But you didn't see him do anything or approach any other people?"

"No, sorry. I pretty much ignored him."

"Gotcha, thanks. Oh, last thing—can you show us exactly where he was standing?"

Marcy pointed to a high line of dunes that separated the beach from the parking lot where we met up with Dad yesterday. "He kept popping up between those dunes. Sorry, guys, but that's all I saw."

"Oh, no problem. You've been a lot of help!"

"Well, I'm glad. Good luck finding the bad guys!"

Marcy ran back to the group of teenagers while the three of us digested what she said. Sammy was the first to speak.

"I don't get it. Why would the Gray Man show up here and hide in the dunes?"

Ali answered him as delicately as she could. "He was

looking for a target, Sammy. Someone he could attack without getting caught. These teenagers would have been able to defend themselves, and even retaliate if he went after one of them. It was one thing for him to take on Brian and the triplets, but this group is much bigger. So, he waited until they weren't looking, and messed with a younger kid that was by himself."

Sammy said, "Oh, okay. Well, at least Marcy's house will be safe from the next hurricane."

I had to respond. "Sammy, listen to yourself. You know the Gray Man only appears right before a storm, but there was no rain at all last night. And Marcy said the other people in her group saw him, too. That's not how the Gray Man does things. He only appears to a couple of people at a time. I'm telling you, something just isn't right about this whole thing!"

"I agree," said Ali, "and I can think of one place we can go to try to start sorting it out." She was staring at the dunes where Marcy said the stranger was hiding. I felt a wave of fright shoot down my spine, because I was never really much of a rule breaker. Even though I knew she wouldn't agree to let this clue go, I had to try.

"Ali, you know I'm with you on this mission, and I'd do just about anything to help. But no one is allowed on the dunes, not even adults! If we get caught, we'll get in *serious* trouble. Why don't we just hang out and see if the Gray Man comes back today?"

Surprisingly, she took a moment to consider her response before shooting me down. "Pete, I really appreciate all of your help so far," she eyed my brother, "and yours, too, Sammy. And I understand that you two want to stay out of trouble. But we're the only ones that can find out who hurt Brian that night, so I can't ignore anything that might lead us to the truth. Maybe the Gray Man dropped something in those dunes that can help us figure this out. Or maybe he left footprints we could recognize again later. I don't know, but I have to at least go look. I can't make you go up there, but I could really use your help."

Yet again, I was sorry for even attempting to slow down Ali's plan. I nodded to Sammy and we started toward the dunes.

It had been less than an hour since we left the house, but the intense morning sun was already taking a serious toll on our energy. It was so humid that the air itself was sticking to our sweaty skin, and it was hard to take a full breath. The wind was still nowhere to be found, leaving us with absolutely no relief except the ocean, which was technically off-limits since there were no adults with us. But apparently the rules did not apply to us today.

We casually walked toward the dunes, each of us observing the people nearby to make sure no one was watching. At the same time, we were inspecting the mounds of sand to identify the best place to climb up. I pointed toward the path that led from the beach to the parking lot, and without a word we took that route. The walkway weaved through the dunes, not up into them, but it would provide the best cover for our quest because the tall dunes would be all around us. We would be hidden from view of anyone except other people walking the path.

We stopped halfway down the path and looked around. The coast was clear. Still silent, Ali took the lead and charged up the tall hill nearest us. My brother and I followed, but Sammy had a hard time getting up the steep slope. It took him a few tries, but he eventually made it to the top.

It was cool to see the beach from this angle. Pawleys is very flat. Our house has a porch that's raised above the sand, but all you can see from there is the water and a small stretch of beach in either direction. From this dune, though, I could see the whole South End spread out before me. Countless umbrellas, chairs, coolers, toys, and people were littered across the sand. At the very tip of the island I saw where the ocean ends and the creek begins, its lazy, curving current running around the back of the South End and up past the parking lot behind us. More people were on its bank, some fishing, some floating, some swimming. From this forbidden castle I felt like the King of Pawleys, looking down over my loyal subjects as they enjoyed my generosity in letting them play on my beach. But I was quickly dethroned, as I realized that every person I could see could very likely see me, too. And we weren't supposed to be up here.

Ali and Sammy had already descended to the inner valley between the dunes. I slid down and joined them. What I hadn't noticed from above was the complex web of pathways down here. It seemed like we could hide in here and run all up and down the South End undetected. The only hard part would be getting out unseen . . . but we would have to figure that out soon enough.

We started across the valley floor and looked for clues. Seeing this immense hiding place, I felt much more confident that we would find something useful here. The Gray Man could have been back here all day yesterday, able to spy on the entire beach until he found the perfect victim. Surely if he was here he would have left some evidence behind. Maybe he was planning to use this as his base all week. In which case, I realized for the first time, he could actually be in here *right now!*

But even as large as the valley was, it didn't take us long to discover it was empty. There were some footprints, and we studied them carefully, but the sand back here was so loose that we couldn't even agree on whether they were from shoes or bare feet. Ali was clearly disappointed, but recovered quickly enough to lead us back to our entry point so we could get out the way we came in. "I want to come back this evening," she said. "He attacked just before dark yesterday. Maybe we can catch him before he hurts anybody else." I nodded agreement.

We struggled to the top of the dune, and I had to pause for one more gaze over my kingdom. I took a deep breath and then slid down to the parking-lot path, and we raced toward the beach. But, as we turned the final corner, I was mortified to see that our way was blocked—by a Beach Patrol officer!

Chapter 11

WE FROZE IN OUR TRACKS AND LOOKED helplessly into the man's face. He was short and heavy, with wavy dark hair and a thick moustache. The Pawleys Beach Patrol does not wear police uniforms, but instead simple navy-blue shorts and white polo shirts with a badge over the chest pocket. He folded his arms and looked down at us through his aviator sunglasses. He didn't say anything for what felt like forever. Dad does this sometimes, too, when he wants me to admit what I did wrong before he even asks me. But we all stood silent, waiting for him to start the lecture.

When he finally did speak, he got right to the point: "You kids mind explaining just what you were doing up in those dunes?"

Sammy, who had been pretty quiet today, was the first of us to answer. "We were looking for the Gray Man!"

Oh great, I thought. Why couldn't Sammy just let Ali and me handle this? I was instantly embarrassed to even be standing next to my brother, much less claim him as a blood relative. And it was even worse than normal this time, since we were specifically trying to leave grown-ups out of our plans. But I knew Ali hated when I treated him that way, and now that he had said it, our best chance of getting out of trouble was to go along and tell a unified story. But Ali was already a step ahead of me.

"We were on the beach and I thought I saw him back in this area. I thought it would be good luck if I caught him, or at least got a closer look, so I started running after him. Pete and Sammy here tried to stop me, but I led them straight over the dunes. I'm sorry, officer. I know we aren't supposed to, but I just had to climb up and try to find him!"

The patrolman stood there. "The Gray Man, huh?" He took off his sunglasses and eyed each of us carefully and deliberately. "Y'all know what the fine is for climbing on the dunes?"

"No, sir," Ali said.

"It's two hundred dollars each. Y'all's little ghost hunt could very well have cost your parents *six hundred bucks.* How do you feel about finding the Gray Man now?"

"I feel like we should stop looking for him, at least in the dunes," Ali replied humbly.

"I think that's a great idea," the officer said. We were all quiet and still for yet another moment. All I could think of was the astronomical amount of trouble I would be in if Dad had to pay $600 for something I knew we shouldn't have done. But I couldn't say no to Ali. I just couldn't. So if we had to pay a fine, I would just tell Dad I would pay him back with my allowance over the next six years, or however long it took. I snuck a peek over at Ali and Sammy, and they were both extremely tense. Clearly, neither of them had gone through the same thought process I did.

Just when I was about to say something, the officer finally spoke again. "Well, I guess I'll let y'all off with a warning this time. But I'm going to be watching for you three, and if I catch you up there again, you won't be so lucky."

"Oh, thank you, officer!" Ali said, "Thank you so much! No, of course we won't go back in there, or on any other dunes for that matter. Sorry again!"

"All right, well, y'all be safe out here," the officer finished, and putting his sunglasses back on, he stepped aside to let us pass. We ran toward the ocean at full speed and then turned toward the jetty, only looking back to see if he was still there. He was, and he was still watching us all the way until we were safely out of his sight on the other side of the rocks.

We stopped running and tried to catch our breath, but the extreme heat and humidity made it nearly impossible. We waded out into the water, again just up to our knees, so we could cool off a little. Once we had recovered from our mad dash, Ali said, "Oh my gosh, you guys, I am so sorry! I know you tried to warn me, Pete, but I had no idea they were *that* strict here!"

"It's okay," I said. "You were right. We had to go in there to look for clues. Even though we didn't find anything, we got away with a warning, so it worked out fine."

"We got lucky," she shot back.

"Lucky, yes. But it was fun."

"Fun?" She smiled. "*You* had *fun* breaking the rules?"

"Well, I don't want to do it again anytime soon. But the view was awesome, and I saw a part of Pawleys I had never seen before. I feel like I know the island better now."

"Well, that certainly is a positive way to look at it. I'm

glad I am helping you have fun on your vacation instead of just making you help me with my mission."

"It's *our* mission, Ali, and I've been having fun helping you." *I would have fun doing anything as long as you were there,* I wanted to say, but didn't. Instead I called to Sammy, "You okay, bro?"

"Yeah, I'm fine, but that was scary!"

"I know. And what's even more scary is now the police might be on to us. Why'd you blurt out that we were looking for the Gray Man before Ali or I could even say anything?"

"Because that was the truth, Pete, and Mom and Dad always say we should tell the truth. Especially when we're talking to grown-ups."

"I know, Sammy, but sometimes when you're a little older, you need to lie to stay out of trouble. It worked out this time because Ali finished telling the story, but next time could you please let us handle things like that?"

Before he could answer, Ali said, "You know, guys, it's not necessarily a bad thing that the officer heard us talk about the Gray Man like that. First of all, you're right, Sammy—it's always good to tell the truth. At least it will be easy to remember if we ever have to tell anyone else what happened today. But think about it. Now if there's another attack, and someone *does* go to the police, it won't be the first time the Beach Patrol will be hearing about the Gray Man this week. And if they put the clues together, then they'll realize that *we just showed them where his hideout is,* even if he doesn't leave anything there when he's gone."

"Wow, that actually does make sense," I said. "I guess you did good, Sammy."

"You *definitely* did good! Now, I'm blistering hot and exhausted. What do you say we go play inside until lunchtime?"

My brother and I nodded and we walked back to the house.

My parents and Ali's parents were sitting together on the beach when we arrived home. Mom asked how our walk was and if we found any Pawleys Shells. We said we had fun, but no luck with the shells. It occurred to me that from my parents' perspective, we had been out shell hunting an awful lot this week with nothing to show for it. I made a mental note that next time we might need to think of another excuse to get away, or actually search and find a Pawleys Shell.

After chatting with our folks for a few minutes, I said I was hot and tired and needed to go inside for a while. Ali and Sammy quickly concurred, and a few minutes later the three of us were alone in the house. We drank some water and crashed in the living room, Sammy in an armchair, Ali and I on opposite ends of the couch. The cold air felt amazing on my skin, and I just sat there with my feet up and my arms spread out, absorbing the relaxation as my body temperature returned to normal. Deep breaths became even deeper. I closed my eyes.

I awoke to Sammy jumping on my still-bare chest and touching his forehead to mine. "Wake up, sleepyhead! We're going crabbing!"

I shoved him off me and took in my surroundings. It took me a minute to remember why I was on the couch, but then I saw Ali asleep on the pillows just two overstuffed cushions away. I continued my survey and saw Mom and Dad in the kitchen gathering the bait and other supplies. Dad caught my eye and whispered, "You better wake her up, son. She won't want to miss this."

I better wake her up, indeed. I stood up and approached her, but quickly realized I had no idea what I was doing. Sure, I had gotten Sammy up plenty of times, and even a few friends when they spent the night at my house. But those were all boys, and it was easy to shove them or start bouncing around like Sammy had just done to me. But I wanted to be careful with Ali. No, not careful—*gentle*. I kneeled down right by her face and leaned over her. She looked very peaceful, her entire body at ease except for her curly red hair, which was strewn out all over the back and the arm of the couch. I slowly reached my hand to her shoulder and gave her just the slightest shake. Nothing happened. I shook her again and whispered, "Ali."

She opened her eyes and smiled when she saw it was me. "Wow, Pete, I need to take you back to Tennessee for the school year. I'd hire you to be my full-time alarm clock."

Once again this girl had scrambled my brain with a simple compliment. I knelt there, perfectly still and mute, for what felt like forever before Dad finally bailed me out. "Come on, kids, everything's ready. Let's go catch some crabs!"

I looked up at Dad and he gave me a wink. I was thankful for the rescue, but at the same time I was completely horrified that my entire family had watched me wake her up like that. There was nothing I could do but get up and head toward the crab dock.

CHAPTER 12

STILL SHIRTLESS FROM THE MORNING, I SLATHERED on some fresh sunscreen as we walked down our short driveway, across the street, and onto the small dock. Sammy and Ali did the same, but Mom and Dad were wearing their normal clothes. Dad started the final preparations: he scooped some creek water into the bucket, unwrapped the bait hooks, and opened up the package of raw, rotten chicken.

"Sammy, you want to try baiting this year?" he asked.

"Ew, no way!" my brother answered, and he ran to Mom and hid behind her.

Dad laughed, cuing Mom, Ali, and me to laugh, too. Dad interrupted us by saying, "What about you, Peter? Want to give it a shot?"

"No, thanks," I said, and then everyone was laughing at me.

"What's so funny?" Ali whispered to me.

"That chicken . . . is so gross . . . you'd smell it on your hands for a week if you touched it!"

She didn't miss a beat. "I'll try it," she said, but Mom, Dad, and Sammy were still laughing and didn't hear her. "I'll try baiting the line," she said a little louder, and the crowd fell silent as my family registered what she was saying. Dad's eyes were impressed as she walked over to him and asked how to do it. He grabbed a hook and a piece of stinky chicken and demonstrated the process on one line, while Ali mimicked his motions on a second rig. Her execution was flawless. My brother and I were still staring in awe when she spun around to show off her work. She smiled proudly, but took no time to gloat. She turned back to Dad and asked, "Now what?"

He showed her how to toss the line into the shallow water and slowly drag it back in. "When it gets close enough that you can see it, look for a crab nibbling on the bait," he told her. "If you see one, call for a net. Do it quietly, though, because you don't want to be too loud and scare them off. Peter, you help her and I'll work with Mom and Sammy."

The three of them walked partway back toward the street and set up off the side of the boardwalk, leaving Ali and me alone at the end. She cast her line, and for a moment everything was quiet. The creek water flowed smoothly beneath the antique wooden supports. A crane flew by. The breeze was warm and salty on my face, and Ali was a wild contrast of tan, carefree summer with fierce concentration on the task at hand.

A thought occurred to me. I peeked back to make sure the others were out of earshot, and then quietly divided Ali's attention. "You know, those footprints in the dunes really did tell us something."

"What's that?" she whispered back, now slowly pulling the line back in.

"They tell us he's real. The Gray Man. I mean, I know he's real, but Tom said he looked like he was floating through the air, like the ghosts you see on TV. If he was floating, then he couldn't have left those footprints, right?"

"Right . . . but those could have been anybody's footprints. Another tourist, or maybe a local who wanted some peace and quiet on the busy beach. It's a good thought, but it doesn't really prove anything."

Of course she was right. We sat there for a few more

minutes as she continued to smoothly inch the bait back toward us.

"Pete," she said, still quiet but now with a little intensity in her voice. "Pete, I think I have one."

I followed her line into the water and found the bait floating just below the surface. Sure enough, a small blue crab was latched onto the bottom of the chicken, shoveling the grossness into his mouth one clawful at a time.

"Net," I called, "net!" But I was too quiet and no one heard me. "Keep it right there under the water and don't move," I said to Ali. Then I jumped up and ran toward Mom and Dad, who were both leaning over the handrail, watching Sammy slowly tug on his line.

Dad eyed me just as I was taking the net out of his hand. "Y'all have one, champ?" he asked, but I was already halfway back to the end of the dock and didn't answer. I peeked over the side; the crab was still there. I lay down with my head and chest out over the water and slowly moved the net toward the surface. I could hear my family's footsteps coming up behind me. Then Dad was lying down next to me on the dock. "Nice and easy, son. Just like I taught you." I lowered my weapon toward the crab and took a deep breath, then in one quick motion sent it scooping into the creek.

It always takes a second to know whether you actually

caught the crab or not. You have to aim for the bait, so if you do it right you end up netting the chicken every time. So, you feel some extra weight even if the crab got away. It's not until you pull it up a little that you can see your bounty.

As I lifted, I could see something wiggling furiously within the mesh. I had it! The scene erupted and a slew of words from Mom, Dad, Sammy, and Ali flooded my ears, freezing me while I tried to process all that was said. Luckily, it was Dad's voice that registered first: "Quick! Move it over to the bucket before he slips out!"

I stood up and swung the net around to the bucket behind me, but I was not fast enough. The crab fell out of the net and landed on the wooden floor, just inches away from Mom's bare feet! She screamed and jumped up onto the bench while the rest of us scurried toward the opposite corner of the dock.

The crustacean raised its claws and surveyed its environment. The humans were now far away, but one still held the net, and the large white bucket loomed distrustfully nearby. The chicken had been dropped and was within a few steps, and the dock's edges were all around, marking the long drop back to the safety of the water.

Dad spoke softly. "Go on, son. You can catch him again. Drop it from straight above him."

I could tell the crab was watching as I tightened my grip and took a tiny step forward. We stood there motionless for a brief moment, standing off like two gunslingers, each waiting for the other to flinch first. I pounced. At my first movement, the crab darted toward the edge, and after two quick steps I swung the net down and covered him. He tried to keep running but was forced to stop. I had him pinned, but I realized I had no idea how to lift him from here—the ring of the net was rigid, so if I tried to turn it up he would have an easy opening to crawl out the other side. I looked to Dad for advice. He was holding the bucket and moving toward the edge of the dock.

"I'll hold this just under the lip of the wood. You slide him straight toward it and push him over the side."

This was crazy! We had never done anything like this before. But Dad was already holding the bucket out over the creek, so I slowly started to move the net flat along the floorboards. When the crab sensed the edge approaching, he tried again to crawl toward it and was quickly met by the bucket. We had our first crab!

Dad and Sammy gave me high-fives, and Mom and Ali gave me hugs. For the second time I felt like the King of Pawleys, and I had demonstrated my mastery of all things beachly to my loyal subjects. It was awesome.

We stayed out crabbing until the tide was too high in

the creek—when the water gets deep, you have to pull the crabs farther off the bottom in order to catch them, and they usually drop off the bait before they reach the surface. Dad had helped Sammy catch a couple of small ones, and Ali and I came close but couldn't snag any more after that first one. We packed up our gear and said goodbye to our catch, then Dad dumped the bucket and its contents back into the creek.

We said goodbye to Ali and reminded her to wash the raw chicken off her hands before she ate anything. She went home, and we went inside for dinner. Steak night. No complaints here, although Mom did make me put a shirt on for the first time all day.

Chapter 13

After dinner, I went out to the front porch and sat in the hammock. Mom came out with her book and sat in a rocking chair next to me. The sun was setting, but there was just enough light for her to read. We sat in silence for a while as the heat finally started to release its hold on the day. The beach was empty, except for a few strolling vacationers and some local sandpipers searching for their dinner. It had been a long day. I started to doze off.

Mom gently called my name. I slowly peeled my eyes open and expected her to tell me to go inside and get in bed. Instead, she simply nodded her head toward the porch next door and continued reading. I followed her gesture and saw Ali and her parents sitting out on their porch. I sat up, somehow wide awake again. They were talking and didn't see me, so I waved a modest wave in their direction. Still nothing. I got up and walked past Mom to their side of the porch and waved again. Now Ali saw me, and her face lit up and she ran to the edge of her porch, as well.

"Hey, Pete! How was your dinner?" she called across the narrow gap between our houses.

"It was great, how was yours?"

"Fine," she answered plainly. "We just ordered pizza." I was shocked, but then I reminded myself that not everyone had the longstanding traditional meals my family holds sacred. Before I could say anything else, I heard Mom whisper from behind me.

"Peter, you two can go down to the beach if you want to. Just stay right in front of our house and don't go in the water."

"Really?" I said eagerly, and called across the way, "Hey, Ali! Want to go down to the beach?"

She smiled big and looked to her dad for permission. He nodded but issued similar limits to those Mom had given me. We both ran down our respective porch steps and met in the sand in between. To my surprise, Brian and Marcy were already down there, looking out over the water, whispering and giggling. I quickly froze, realizing Ali and I really had nothing to do. We couldn't go walking, we couldn't swim, and it was getting too dark to play games. I tilted my head back to think, and when I did I could see the moon and the first few stars of the evening starting to twinkle above us. I followed the remaining sunlight back toward the creek and saw a beautiful red sky. Right between our houses, the last lingering disc of the sun was setting behind the trees.

"Let's watch the sunset," I said, and she turned toward the west and gasped at the view.

We stood there together for a minute or two, and then something happened. Ali nudged closer to me, and closer still, until our shoulders were touching. I felt her arm against my arm. Then, she slowly slipped her hand into mine and interlaced our fingers.

We were holding hands.

To describe how I felt will sound like I completely blacked out. I didn't, but my heart was racing so fast I thought it would stop. I was sweating, and my vision blurred until all I could comprehend were the bright reds and oranges of the sunset gashing through the oncoming night. I had never held hands with a girl before—no girl back home had ever wanted to—so I was definitely nervous. And yet, I was also . . . comfortable. Ali made it feel so easy, so natural. We stood there together until the sun was all the way down, and then kept standing there, staring at the moonlit shadows of Pawleys Island.

I was drawn out of my trance by the sound of a screen door closing. A member of one of our families had either come outside or gone back in. I started counting the seconds until one of us was called inside for bedtime.

Ali must have also heard the door and come to the same conclusion that our time was short. She said, "This was very nice, Pete. Thanks for inviting me out." She gave my hand a squeeze and then let go, and at that very moment Mom called me to come in.

"I had fun, too. Goodnight," I said, and we turned toward our separate stairways.

But then something else happened.

I had only taken a few steps toward my house when I peeked back to steal one last glance at Ali for the night. My eye was caught by something moving on the jetty. I spun back and called to Ali and pointed her toward the rocks. She was instantly by my side again and asked what it was, and our lovestruck evening turned to horror as I came to realize what I was seeing.

"Ali . . . it's . . . *him!*"

"Who?"

"*THE GRAY MAN!*"

I was terrified, but Ali showed her strength yet again. She grabbed my arm and ran straight toward him. We breezed by Brian and Marcy, and I quickly called to Mom that I needed a few more minutes before I came up.

The night sky had defeated the fiery sunset, and the beach was glowing in moonlight. Ali ran without concern toward the shimmering water and the dark phantom. We lined up in his path and waited for his approach.

As he got nearer, I examined his clothing. It was just as the triplets had said: an old military uniform with a cape and a wide-brimmed hat, all gray. But he didn't appear to "float," like Tom had said. He looked like a normal person just running down the shoreline. I searched under his hat for any facial features, but all I could make out was a sinister, plastic-y grin. I shivered in fear.

But this was wrong. All my life I had learned to love this compassionate spirit, but now that I finally saw him, my fright was heightening with every step he took in our direction. We should be safe with him, but we were not. I braced myself for an attack, but he flew right by me.

I spun around and saw Brian there, and my dream from just last night came rushing back into my mind. This time I didn't wait, though; I instantly started running toward Brian to protect him and see what the ghost would really say for himself.

When the Gray Man reached Ali's brother, he extended one arm out to his side and clotheslined Brian without missing a stride. Instead of following him to the ground and continuing the attack, he simply laughed a husky laugh and kept running. Marcy, Ali, and I were quickly at Brian's side, kneeling in the sand and asking if he was okay. He was. Then Ali asked the question we'd been trying to answer all week: "Brian, is that the same guy that beat you up Sunday night?"

"Yeah, that's him."

Marcy piped in, "Oh my gosh, you guys! That's the creep I was telling you about this morning! The one that was, like, spying on us from behind the dunes!"

I looked at Ali. She was already looking at me with the fiercest eyes I've ever seen. I summoned all the courage I could and then nodded, and in perfect unison we stood up and took off chasing after the attacker.

The encounter had not gone exactly as it had in my dream, but after running only a few strides I remembered one final detail. I paused. *Yes, I have to at least go look.*

I darted back to where Brian and Marcy were still on the ground and scanned the sand around where they were sitting. And there it was.

Ali called back, "What are you doing, Pete? Come on!"

I quickly reached down, grabbed the shell, and started running back toward the Gray Man.

We chased him for about a jetty and a half—not too terribly far, considering Mom had told me to stay in front of our house AND had just called me to come inside for the night (and to think, last year I wouldn't have even *considered* breaking her rules). But we were getting winded, and after our extremely long day I knew we couldn't chase him forever. Actually, I take that back—Ali really might have. She was more determined now than I had ever seen her. She sprinted at her top speed for the entire length of our run, only slowing down when our target slowed ahead of us. I didn't know what we would do if he came back and attacked us, but he acted like he didn't know we were behind him. When he came to a full stop, we hurried up under a nearby porch so we could continue watching but stay hidden from his view.

He stood still in the sand for a moment, catching his breath or thinking of what to do next. We were only one house away and the moon was bright, so we were able to carefully observe his every move. Then it happened: He reached up to his hat and removed it, then pulled upwards on his hair and his entire face rose with it. He balled up the elaborate mask and stuffed it inside the hat, then turned toward the house next to our hiding spot and started walking toward the porch.

My stomach dropped as soon as I saw his real face. *It was Derek Henderson!*

I didn't say anything to Ali at first, because any noise could have drawn his attention. We waited and watched as he walked up the steps and into the house, and then I let loose.

"I can't believe it! All this time we think we're chasing ghosts, when really it's just plain-old, mean-old Derek dressed up in some stupid costume. I should have known he was behind all of this! I thought he wasn't here because he's not in the same house as before. It never even occurred to me that he just got a different house this year. . . . Why didn't I think of that? Oh man, everything that's happened all week makes perfect sense now. It's the same stuff he does every year, only this time he dressed up so he could have his fun and not get in trouble. And to think, I actually believed that the Gray Man was hurting people!"

Ali put her hands on my shoulders and looked firmly into my eyes. "Pete! Stop it! This isn't your fault! No one could have guessed it was him. And even if you had suspected Derek was here, tonight was the first time we've seen him all week. And the only reason we saw him tonight was because . . . because you asked me out. I mean, you invited me to watch the sunset! If we hadn't been down here, we might never have gotten to the bottom of this. So don't be hard on yourself. You're the one who solved the mystery!"

I smiled, and not one of those forced, I-guess-you're-right smiles. This one was genuine, from the heart. Once again, Ali had used her magical way of making me feel good about myself, even when I did absolutely nothing to deserve it. She lowered her hands and her left one caught my right, and we walked home slowly.

Brian and Marcy were already gone when we got to the foot of my stairs. Ali gave me a hug and said, "One more thing, Pete. Back there you said you actually believed the Gray Man was hurting people?"

"Right."

She shook her head. "Wrong. You never believed that. Not for a single minute."

I was struck by another forgotten memory of my dream. I had asked the Gray Man why he was hurting people. *You already know the answer.* He and Ali were right: I *knew* it wasn't really him!

We said goodnight and I walked up to the porch. Mom was still sitting there, although it had gotten too dark for her to read. Dad was still inside. He was undoubtedly the tougher disciplinarian, but Mom could hold her own when it came to getting me in trouble. She was also much more lenient, though, and with a stern "Goodnight, Peter," she ushered me into the house.

My room was pitch black, but I managed to sneak past my sleeping brother and collapse into bed. I fell asleep to the sweet smell of rotten chicken on my right hand.

Chapter 14

"Peter? Wake up, son. It's time."

I awoke to find Dad sitting on the side of my bed and the first beams of morning sunlight echoing through my room. It was Thursday. I sat up sleepily and peered at Sammy, still under the covers with Alfonso by his side.

Dad spoke again. "Come on, champ, you need to take a shower. Mom already has breakfast going, and then we'll get out of here."

Of course! As much as there is to do at the beach, there's also tons of cool stuff right up the road from where we stay. We always take Thursday off the island to go explore the nearby shops, restaurants, and whatever else we can find. In recent years we've played mini golf, hiked through botanical gardens, and checked out a huge aquarium. Dad says the older we get, the more options we'll have, but I've never been disappointed in our adventures so far.

I got up and took a shower—my first since Monday—and dressed in khaki shorts and a polo shirt. Sammy did the same, and then we all ate breakfast together. We were just about to leave when someone knocked on the front door. It was probably Ali, and my heart sank as I realized I was ditching her. We would be gone all day, and she'd be on her own with nothing to do but get made fun of by Brian. And she'd have no help if Derek decided to cause more trouble. I offered to answer the knock so I could break the news to her myself.

But when I opened the door, I was met with a surprise. There was a girl standing there, but I hardly recognized her. Her windblown red hair was tame and clean. Her face was highlighted by red lipstick and blue eye makeup, but not too much. Gone was the bathing suit—which is all I had ever seen her wear—and in its place was a white dress with yellow flowers and a rounded collar. She had also switched out her flip-flops for classy sandals that also had yellow flowers on them. All I could think was, *Wow.*

"Thanks, you too," she said shyly, and I honestly didn't know if I had said anything or if she just read my mind. But either way, I was confused. Why was she dressed up when we were the ones leaving for the day?

Mom greeted our guest before I could ask. "Good morning, Ali. Nice dress! You ready to go?"

"Yes, ma'am," Ali replied, and she gave me a big smile. "Your mom talked to my mom last night and invited me to go along with y'all today. Surprise!"

Well, there's my answer. Before I knew it, I was squished between Ali and Sammy in the backseat of our car, and we were off.

Our first stop was the Hammock Shops Village. This collection of about twenty local stores is situated on the mainland not far off the North Causeway. They have all kinds of souvenirs, books, toys, decorations for your house, and yummy things to eat. We followed Mom and Dad through a couple of boring grown-up stores, but then Dad bought us some Pawleys T-shirts—Ali, too—and we watched the hammock makers spin their white-cotton ropes into comfortable lazy-day lounging supplies. That was pretty cool.

After that, we climbed back in the car and continued on. It seemed like we were driving for a while, but we were all in a good mood and talked about random stuff as we watched the palm trees and surf shops go by. When the signs said we were close to Myrtle Beach, I got really excited. It's a big vacation city that attracts people from all over the South, and there's tons to do there. The beach itself is much busier than Pawleys, and I've never seen any houses, just hotels. So I would never want to spend a whole week there, but the fun stuff makes it worth a day trip. We parked in a busy parking lot and when we got out, we saw a wide, busy boardwalk stretched out ahead of us for miles. It was jam-packed with people, and both sides were lined with shops, games, and every kind of food you could imagine. It was impressive, but a bit overwhelming at the same time. Where should we start? I was about to ask Ali what she wanted to do but Dad spoke up first.

"Now, guys, I know this place looks like fun, and it will be. But you see how many people are here. We absolutely have to stay together. We'll take turns choosing what to do, so just be patient and I promise everybody will get to do everything they want. Deal?"

"Deal!" I shouted, and I heard Ali and Sammy echo.

"Good," Dad continued. "Okay, my turn first. I want something to eat. Let's see . . . who wants funnel cakes?"

We screamed agreement and could barely hold in our excitement as we followed Dad to the nearby food stand.

We gorged ourselves on the fried goodness, washing it down with ice-cold lemonade served in tall, swirly goblets. We walked on. The carnival atmosphere was breathtaking. For Mom's turn, she found a leatherwork store that was actually pretty cool. Ali, Sammy, and I tried on hats and jackets while Mom shopped the handbags and Dad looked at belts. Before long we were back outside, and it was Sammy's turn. But he was too overwhelmed and couldn't choose right away, so we walked the endless pathway and found new options at every turn.

He eventually found a playground and said he wanted to play on it for his turn. Mom and Dad sat down on a nearby bench to watch, and Ali and I joined my brother even though the playset was definitely built for younger kids. We ran around for a minute and then climbed to the top of the structure, and that's when we saw it: back toward the parking lot but tucked away off the main boardwalk was a jumble of tracks, towers, carts, and lights that unmistakably signified an amusement park. There was a small entrance not far back from where we were. I'm not sure how I had missed it on our walk just now, but from this higher view, it was clear.

Ali was excited. "Pete! That looks awesome! Let's go in there and ride some rides!"

"Ha, yeah right. Dad will never let us."

"What do you mean? He said we could each choose whatever we want. It's either your turn or mine after this. Let's tell him we both want to go in there!"

"Ali, don't get me wrong, that place does looks cool. I want to go, but I *know* my Dad won't let us. First of all, Sammy's probably too little to ride any of the rides, so he'll say that's not fair to my brother. Also, I'm guessing the rides cost a lot of money, so we would hardly get to do anything even if he *did* let us go in there. Not to mention that we already walked past it. If he was okay with it, he would have pointed it out to Sammy and asked if he wanted to check it out for his turn. I'm telling you, it's not even worth asking."

"Well then, maybe we just won't ask."

"What is that supposed to mean?"

"It means, let's sneak away right now and go in there when your parents aren't looking!"

"You're insane! Do you know how much trouble I would be in once they found out? And they *would* find out, wouldn't they, Sammy?"

Sammy, who had told on me for everything I had ever done wrong, stood there and smiled. "Not if I get to go with you," he said.

"No," I said strongly. "Absolutely not going to happen."

"Why not?" Ali asked crossly. It had been a while since I had seen her protect my brother like this, but yet again, it was two against one.

I sighed. Dad had been in and out of his trance all week; maybe he was in a good enough mood to let this slide? And come to think of it, Sammy had actually covered for me when Dad grilled us for being gone too long the day we met the triplets.

"Okay, but how are we going to slip away without them noticing we're gone?" I asked.

Ali was quick to respond. "I have an idea. Do your parents know how Sammy plays Tag?"

"Yes."

"Perfect. Let's run around for a minute and then stop right in front of them. I'll ask if y'all want to play Tag, loud so they can hear me. Sammy, you'll be It first. When you go to hide, run over behind that sign by the playground entrance and wait for us there. Pete and I will run around for a few more minutes, keeping an eye on your parents. When they're not looking we'll join you behind the sign. From there we have a clear path to the boardwalk, and we can run to the other side where all the people will keep us hidden. We can run down to the amusement park and just come back pretty quick. Your folks will never even know we're gone."

"Sounds good!" Sammy whispered, happy to be in on the conspiracy. I just nodded, and as we climbed down I wondered how this girl was able to repeatedly convince me to do things that I would never do on my own. Things like this, that I would come to regret.

We sprung our plan and it worked flawlessly, and in only a few minutes we were running down the boardwalk toward the entrance hidden just a few storefronts away.

Chapter 15

IF THE BUZZ OF THE BOARDWALK WAS breathtaking, the air inside the theme park was pure energy. Everywhere we looked there were lights flashing and roller-coaster cars whooshing by. Gusts of wind from the ocean brought to our noses an intoxicating mixture of popcorn and hydraulic grease, and our ears were assaulted equally by electronic games, rickety rides, and laughter. The three of us bumped our way through the crowd to explore the area, marveling at something new with every step.

Unfortunately, I had been right: None of the rides or games were free, so we couldn't do anything except watch.

But as we stood by the Ferris wheel, I tried to imagine the view from the top, with the busy streets below and the Atlantic Ocean spread out just beyond the fairground gates. I wondered if I could see all the way to Pawleys from there.

We wandered the area for a few more minutes and then decided to go back. This was incredible, but we really would be in deep trouble if Dad noticed we were gone from the playground. We were walking back toward the entrance when I spotted someone in the crowd, and stopped cold. Just ahead of us, standing in line for a roller coaster, was Derek.

I couldn't believe it. Just yesterday I was certain I would never have to see him again for the rest of my life. But now I had seen him twice, and discovered that he was once again to blame for all of my problems. I gently grabbed Ali and Sammy by their shoulders and we all stopped walking, and they followed my eyes to identify our nemesis ahead.

"Guys, I don't want him to see us. Let's go around this way and get back to the playground," I said, and I tried to make for a nearby walkway.

But as always, Ali had other plans. Her eyes were sharp and vengeful. After all, he was the one that beat Brian up. "Let's get him in trouble, right here and now," she said slyly.

I knew there was no use trying to talk her down this time, but I had to at least urge her to make it snappy. However much trouble we got him into, it would be nothing compared to Dad's wrath if he caught us here. "What can we do that won't take too long?" I asked.

She whispered the scheme to us, and I didn't like it because it put Sammy at risk. But my brother jumped at the opportunity to play a large role, so he went to work.

The plan was simple and shouldn't have taken long at all. My brother snuck over to where Derek was standing and blended himself into the line right behind our enemy. It had to be Sammy that went, because Derek definitely would have recognized me, and I wouldn't let Ali go near him. She and I tucked ourselves behind a hotdog stand to watch and give Sammy the signal. When Derek was close to the front of the line, we started looking around for an authority figure—a cop, a Beach Patrol officer, or even just a carnival staffer. We saw one at the perfect time, when Derek was only two spots back from his turn on the ride. Ali and I waved at Sammy in unison, his cue to turn on the tears.

Sammy's performance was nothing short of brilliant. He started crying, and not just a little whimper; this was all-out bawling on a grand scale, complete with stomping feet and real tears forming rivers down his cheeks. The busy crowd took notice—even Derek—and within a moment, Sammy was approached by a security guard that we'd seen nearby. When asked what was wrong, my brother pointed up at Derek in dramatic fashion and shouted, *"He cut in line!"*

The security guard put an arm around Sammy's shoulders and then addressed Derek, whose face was an epic combination of denial and confusion.

"Well, how 'bout it, tough guy?" he asked.

Derek did his best to protest, but Sammy kept his charade going in masterful form. Finally the guard had heard enough. "All right, pal, let's go. The park rules say no cutting in line. I'm gonna have to ask you to leave."

It was the exact result we were going for. Ali and I beamed with our victory and shared a hug, then we came out of our hiding spot to get Sammy out of there and go back to the playground.

That's when everything started going wrong.

Derek was fuming mad and lunged at my brother, but luckily the security guard caught him and took him to the ground. Sammy started running toward us, and Derek watched as he came our way and buried his face in my arm. When he saw me, his eyes went wild and he started to shout.

"Petey-Weety! Are you kidding me right now? This was because of *you?* Oh man, you're dead, you hear me? You better watch your back when we get back to Pawleys. Getting me kicked out of here was the worst mistake of your life. You're gonna—"

"That's about enough out of you!" the guard interrupted. But he, too, had watched Sammy run over to me, and as another guard came and grabbed Derek, the first responder made his way over to us. "You okay, kiddo?" he asked Sammy. My brother nodded. "Good. Don't worry about that guy. We get meanies like him in here all the time. And you don't look big enough to ride that coaster, anyway. Why don't you stick with the kiddy rides from now on, okay, buddy?" Sammy nodded again, and then the guard asked us the absolute last question we wanted to hear. "So, where are your parents?"

I was fossilized with fear. We hadn't thought this far ahead in our plan, but I should have known we couldn't pull a stunt like this without answering for it. When none of us replied to the guard, he said, "Hm, alrighty, three lost kids. Come with me."

He took us to a small office in the back of the ticket booth at the entrance. He asked us our names and our parents' names, where we were from, and where we were staying. Then he asked us where we had last seen our folks.

"You mean the playground across from the Fun Maze up the boardwalk?" He sounded truly shocked.

"Yes, sir," I answered.

"And did your parents know you were coming over here?"

The pit in my stomach was coming on fast. I took a deep breath. "No, sir. They don't know we're here."

"Oh, that's just perfect." He leaned over to the back of the desk and picked up a very official-looking walkie-talkie. He spoke some jargon into it, but I could understand my parents' names and their last known location. An officer on the other end answered, saying she was already with my parents and had been looking for us, and would bring them to the office.

All I could think was, *Well, everybody has to die sometime.*

Chapter 16

MOM WAS THE FIRST TO RUSH INTO the office. She pulled all three of us into her arms and thanked God and the security guard at least a thousand times each. The guard was very polite in return and told the brief story of what had transpired, but he did say they needed to keep a better eye on us. This prompted Dad to speak.

"Oh, that won't be a problem, officer." He had been standing just inside the door, still as a stone, watching Mom hug us and listening to the guard's story. I couldn't even look him in the eye.

When we left the office, Dad started walking without a

word. We were to follow him. Sammy held Mom's hand and I held Ali's, but all five of us were silent. Dad led us back to the car. We got in and started the journey back to Pawleys. It was a solid ten minutes before Dad finally unleashed his fury.

"What I don't understand, Peter, is what on *earth* made you think running off like that was okay? I mean, I had one rule. *One* rule when we got here! What was it, son?"

"That we stay together."

"That's right. And what was the second part of that? Huh? That everybody would get their turn to pick what we do. Do you remember me saying that?"

"Yes, sir."

"Well then surely you see why I'm confused, right? I gave you one rule, and I told you we could do whatever you wanted. So I can't *imagine* what was going through your head when you decided to break that *one rule*! Can you explain that to me?"

"Dad, I—"

"It was all my fault, Mr. Prince," Ali interrupted. "We saw the roller coasters from the top of the playground, and it was my idea to—"

"*You stay out of this, Alison!*" Dad shouted. "You don't get to stand up for him this time. Regardless of your bad influence, I expect Peter to make better decisions than that."

"Dad, leave her alone! You're right, I shouldn't have done it and I'm sorry."

"Sorry's not going to cut it this time, son! Do you have any idea what kind of crazy people are out there, that could have done something terrible to you? You could have been kidnapped, beaten up, or even killed! And the fact that you put Sammy at risk, too . . . I just don't even know *what* to think!"

At this, Mom gently moved her hand onto Dad's shoulder and softly raised her eyebrows to him, her standard signal that he'd made his point and it was time to lighten up. At the same time, Ali squeezed my hand in the seat between us.

But Dad wasn't finished.

"You want to know the worst part of this, Peter? All you had to do was ask, and we all could have gone in there together. You might have even convinced me to pay for some rides and games. But what did you do instead? *You betrayed my trust,* scared your mother to death, and put yourself, your brother, and someone else's daughter that *I* am responsible for in a dangerous situation. What would you have done if that security guard hadn't been there? Who knows what kind of sick people are out at tourist places like that? But again, you let someone you've known for less than a week convince you to ignore your own judgment, the judgment I've been teaching you *your entire life*."

Ali jumped in again. "Mr. Prince, if you'd *please* just let me explain—"

"*I told you to stay out of this!* You can explain whatever you want to your parents when we get home. For now, I'm *still* trying to figure out exactly what my son was thinking through all this. Well, Peter? *What were you thinking?*"

"Dad, I said I'm sorry, okay? I was just trying to have a little fun."

"*A little fun?* So, getting to choose what the family did wasn't enough *fun* for you? Look, I'm glad you've made a new friend this year, but if Alison is going to be pressuring you to break my rules, then maybe you two shouldn't play together anymore."

I felt Ali's hand tighten her grip on mine again. I had had enough of Dad's pummeling, but this little squeeze gave me just the fuel I needed.

"*Dad, stop it!* You said it yourself, this was *my* decision, not hers! If you want to punish *me* for that, fine. But you can't make us stop being friends. And . . . and you can't talk to her like that! She's not a bad influence, she's the best friend I've ever had! You think I'm always going to be this perfect little angel. Well, maybe I'm tired of your precious rules! Have you ever thought of that? You yell at me for even the smallest mistake, and it's just . . . *exhausting* trying to keep up with them all! I wish just once you'd let something go, let me do something wrong without getting blasted for it. And another thing—stop calling her 'Alison.' She likes to go by 'Ali.' And while we're at it . . . I want to go by 'Pete' now."

I was shaking, my face was hot, and even though I didn't feel the tears falling, I could tell I had cried. I had *never in my life* talked to my father like that, and I was suddenly terrified of how he might respond. I could tell everyone else was thinking the same thing as I watched Ali, Sammy, and Mom shift their shocked faces toward the driver's seat and brace for what was to come.

But nothing came. I could hear Dad breathing heavily, his knuckles white from his tightened grip on the steering wheel. His eyes pierced me through the rearview mirror, and I could tell he wanted to keep going. But, after a few deep breaths, all he said was, "When we get back to the house, you're going straight to your room for the rest of the day. Understand?"

I nodded. Only then did I release Ali's hand, and when I did, I noticed that Sammy had been squeezing my other hand as well.

We stopped to eat dinner at this seafood place we go to

almost every year. I'm usually pretty excited to eat there, but all I wanted to do was get back to Pawleys. The five of us ate almost completely in silence.

When we got back to the house, Dad sent Ali home and me to my room. I collapsed into bed. The soothing sound of the waves outside tried to calm me down, but I was still upset. I was upset with everybody. I could not *believe* the way Dad yelled at me in front of Ali, or the way he yelled at Ali, for that matter. And Mom just let him! I know she tried to make him stop, but she could have tried a little harder, and I think he would have listened to her. And for the first time all week, I was upset with Ali. Sneaking off and messing with Derek were *both* her ideas, and they really were not good ones. What was I going to say to her tomorrow? Was she at her house right now getting yelled at by her parents? Despite my frustration, I hoped she wasn't.

And I was upset with myself. Although I hated the way Dad talked to me, I had to admit his message was right. I had been so eager to please Ali and try something new that I forgot everything I had learned, and put us all in a terrible situation. I really should have known better.

I started thinking about Sammy. He was not involved with the scheming, but he went along with our plans and certainly played a major role against Derek. Surely he would be hearing from Dad, too. I just hoped it wasn't as serious as what I endured in the car. Just then, I heard my father's voice through the bedroom door. It was muffled, but I know Dad, and I could imagine exactly what he said to Sammy:

"Now, son, you're not completely off the hook here. I know it's hard to say 'no' when your brother wants to do something fun, but as you grow up you'll have to learn to stand up for yourself when your friends make bad decisions. You need to learn from Peter's mistakes—especially this one—and figure out for yourself what's right and wrong. Then, the even harder part will be finding the courage to speak up when you might not want to. I know you're not old enough to get all that, so your only punishment is to stay inside for the rest of the evening. But promise me you'll think about this, and I promise you you'll understand it more and more the older you get. Okay, sport?"

I heard them walk to the kitchen table and start playing UNO with Mom. Before long they were laughing like nothing had happened. Their game went on for a while, but it was getting close to bedtime. I heard Dad plop on the sofa and my brother climb into his lap, and Dad started reading Sammy a book. That's when I heard a knock on my bedroom door.

It was Mom.

"Honey, can I talk to you for a minute before Sammy comes in for bed?" she asked gently.

"Yes, ma'am."

I sat up in bed as she closed the door behind her, then she sat down next to me and gave me a hug. I lost it. I buried my face in her shoulder and cried harder than I could remember crying in a long time. She sat there and held me tight until I finally pulled away, took a few deep breaths, and looked her in the eyes.

"I'm sorry, Mom. I know I shouldn't have done that today. But why does he have to be so hard on me all the time? And in front of Ali! I just . . . I was so embarrassed!"

"I know, honey. Between you and me, I don't like it when he yells like that, either. But he does it because he loves you."

"What? That doesn't make any sense."

"Sure, it does. He wants you to grow up to be a responsible man and take care of yourself and your family. And I hate to say it, but the only way to do that is to learn how to make good decisions. When you make mistakes as a kid, what's the worst thing that happens? You get yelled at and maybe grounded. But when you're an adult, those consequences can be much worse. So, it's really important that Dad and I teach you how to do things the right way, and that means telling you when you've done something wrong. And when you do something *really* wrong . . . we have to make sure you understand exactly what the problem was, and what you should have done differently."

"But can't I figure that out on my own? I mean, I just told you that I know I made a bad choice. Isn't that enough?"

"No, because here's the key—there's a big difference between *knowing* what's right and *doing* what's right. Everything that comes to you in life will be the result of your *actions*, not your thoughts. So, it's good that you can recognize that you made a bad decision, but you still went through with it. You ran off and nearly started a fight, so you have to accept your punishment for that."

Just then, the door opened and Sammy walked in. I gave Mom another big hug and she got up, kissed us both, and said goodnight.

When Sammy was snuggled in, I turned off the lamp between our beds and the room was dark. I lay there thinking of what Mom had said and trying my best to understand it. I *do* know right from wrong, and I do want to be a good grown-up one day. But I still just didn't get why Dad had to discipline me so harshly. So I did something I shouldn't have. Talk to me about it calmly and I'll listen much better than if you scream.

These thoughts played over and over in my head until I started dozing off. The last thing I heard was Sammy's voice saying, "I had fun today, Pete. Sorry you got in trouble. I love you."

"I love you, too," I managed to reply.

Chapter 17

I'll never know why Sammy picked that Friday, of all days, to take his stuffed elephant down to the beach with him. None of us thought anything of it at the time, but looking back now, it's obvious that that one decision led to the events that finally put an end to our troubles. And changed our lives forever.

Sammy perched Alfonso on the bottom stair of our porch so the elephant could "watch" us play. I had avoided Dad all morning, even skipping breakfast, and I planned to stay outside as much as possible. I didn't want to spend my last full day here rehashing yesterday's argument.

So, Ali met us out front and we hung out on the beach for most of the day. Mom and Dad seemed to rotate from the porch to the beach to inside the house, which worked out great because we were supervised, but I could still keep away from Dad. Tim, Tom, and Davy Ray stopped by and hung out with us for a while, and we swam, played Tag, and drew funny pictures in the sand, all under Alfonso's watchful eye.

By lunchtime I was starving, but luckily Ali said we could go to her house to eat since my family had been feeding her all week. Afterward, Mrs. Baxter gave us fresh coats of sunscreen, and we went back outside to play the day away.

Late in the afternoon, some really big storm clouds popped up over the ocean. We kept playing. The clouds quickly grew and came ashore, and before long the beach was dark and windy. When the rain started we ran up to our porch, grabbed some towels, and sat down to watch the storm until dinner was ready; tonight we'd have a fantastic combination of shrimp, sausage, corn, and potatoes, known as a low-country boil. Sammy sat in a rocking chair and Ali hopped into the hammock next to me. Soon it was pouring rain, and we just sat there, wiped out from a long day in the sun.

That's when it happened.

A dark figure appeared over the jetty and came running

along the beach toward our house. I could tell right away that it was Derek dressed in his Gray Man costume. He passed Ali's house and then mine, apparently on some mission of no-good that thankfully did not involve us. But just when we thought we were in the clear, he stopped. Something had caught his attention. He walked toward our house and stopped again at the bottom of our stairs. Then he bent over, picked something up, and ran off again.

Sammy shrieked, "*Alfonso!*" and before we could react, he was running at full speed down the stairs and out into the driving rain. Ali and I tumbled out of the hammock and ran after him, but he had a good head start. By the time we got to the sand, Derek was at least three houses away. Sammy was well behind him but running at full speed, determined to rescue his elephant at any cost. It wasn't until I was out in the rain that I realized how bad the storm really was. The raindrops were big and fell hard on my skin. A bright flash of lightning struck over the ocean, and thunder rumbled so loud it seemed to shake the sand under my feet. The strong wind made it difficult to run very fast, but Ali and I caught up with my brother and I grabbed his shoulder from behind. I had to shout so he could hear me over the screaming wind.

"Sammy! It's raining too hard! We need to go back to—"

"Let go of me!" he interrupted, and his rain-soaked shoulder slipped out of my grasp. He kept running.

Ali and I exchanged a quick look, and then continued after him. When we caught him again, Ali shouted, "Sammy! We'll find Alfonso in the morning! Your dad will get mad if he finds us out in this weather!"

That made him pause for a moment. He knew he got off easy yesterday and shouldn't press his luck. But the look on his face was determined, and he yelled, "I don't care! He can get mad if he wants to! I can't let Derek hurt Alfonso!" He took off again.

I looked ahead to locate Derek. As I broadened my view, the scene around me finally sunk in, and I was genuinely scared. It was almost high tide. No one else was on the beach. The storm was creating waves bigger than I had ever seen at Pawleys, and they made loud crashes as they pounded into the jetties. The sky was black and the wind was relentless, its howling broken only by the bone-shaking thunder. The rain was like a constant barrage of icy pinpricks all over my body, and I felt myself shivering cold.

This is really dangerous, I thought. *We need to get back to the house.*

But my brother was still sprinting ahead. Through the sheets of rain I could barely make out Derek's outline. He was at least five houses away, but it looked like he had stopped, or at least slowed down. In a final attempt to stop Sammy, I ran up to him again and this time grabbed him in a bear hug around his waist, lifting him off the ground and turning back toward the house. But he squirmed his way loose, and without a word he was running up the beach again.

I shouted to Ali, "Go back to the house and get my dad! I'll stay with Sammy and deal with Derek!"

She was squinting in the rain, but I could still read the concern on her face. "You sure?"

It was a good question. *Am I sure?* Our scheme at the amusement park was the closest I had ever come to standing up to him. What was I going to say? Was I willing to fight with him in the middle of what had to be a tropical storm? But Sammy definitely couldn't do it, and he obviously wasn't going to let up until he had his elephant back. So, it was up to me. I gave her a thumbs-up, and quickly turned back toward my brother so she couldn't reply.

By the time I caught up with Sammy for the fourth time, I could tell Derek had stopped right at the edge of the water near the jetty. As we approached him, I could feel the spray of the waves as they collided with the rocks. The storm was not letting up. We stopped right in front of him, Sammy and me side by side against the teenager. He held up Alfonso and gave us a sneer.

"Looking for this?"

"Give it back!" Sammy shouted, and jumped up, trying to grab the elephant. Derek laughed and jerked it away just before Sammy reached it. My brother jumped again, but this time Derek used his free hand to push Sammy down on his back. At the same moment a wave rushed up and Sammy was covered by salt water. He flailed, trying to get his feet back under him, and I reached down and grabbed his arm and helped him stand. He was coughing and disoriented, obviously taken off guard by the massive wave. As the water retreated, he stepped back from the shoreline and leaned over, salt water dripping from his mouth and nose.

"Sammy! Are you okay?" I asked him.

He didn't answer. He just looked at me and sat down in the sand, gasping for air between the raindrops. I felt a rush of relief, but then a new emotion overtook me. I clenched my fists and turned back to Derek. I wasn't shivering anymore; in fact, I felt like my body was on fire. Lightning lit the sky and I could see a calm satisfaction on Derek's face, like he had *enjoyed* hurting my brother. This was going to end right now. I marched up to him and stared directly into his eyes.

"You just crossed the line, Derek!" I said. "You can mess with me all you want, but you don't touch my brother. He could have drowned!"

Another wave rushed under our feet, and a loud clap of thunder rattled the earth.

"Oh, really? Well, just what are you gonna do about it, Petey-Weety? He deserved it after that little stunt he pulled in Myrtle Beach yesterday. I figure we're almost even now . . . *almost*. Just remember, this is my beach, and I can do whatever I want. This little elephant means nothing to me, just like you mean nothing to me. Same with your brother and your little red-haired girlfriend. I was just going to toss this up in the dunes and make you get in trouble again, but if you're gonna talk back to me, I think it might just have to go away forever."

He faced the ocean and took a few steps into the waves. He cocked his arm back like he was going to throw Sammy's most prized possession into the water. I shouted, "No! Don't! I'm warning you!"

Another flash of lightning revealed an evil smile on Derek's face, and before I could stop him, he launched Alfonso into the blackness of the night.

My rage boiled over. I lunged toward him with my fists flying, my eyes blind to everything except the sudden look of surprise on his face. But before I made contact, I was grabbed from behind and spun around. I found myself face to face with Ali, her eyes wide and her palms facing me in a defensive pose, probably to make sure I didn't hit her by accident. She slowly moved her hands toward mine and closed them gently around my fists, and my anger instantly melted away. She pulled me close and whispered into my ear. Even through the violent storm I heard her clearly: "He's not worth it, Pete."

I sighed and lowered my fists. The rain was pelting my face, driven almost horizontally by the unyielding wind. Another wave devoured the jetty and rushed up past our knees. Lightning crashed and thunder followed. I looked over at Sammy, who had stood up again and was walking toward us, his eyes trained steadily on the water as he entered. When he reached us I put my arm around his shoulder, pulled him in close, and then lowered my hand to my side. He slipped his hand into mine, and I realized my other hand was still holding Ali's. I gave them both a squeeze, and we looked at each other in complete confidence and understanding, yet wholly vulnerable in the ferocious storm. As we stood there, I thought I saw another figure walking on the beach, but it was too far away to tell who it was through the dense rain.

Ali was right. Derek wasn't worth it. But this still had to end, so we turned toward him all at once. Instantly I was reminded of just how grave our situation was. He was laughing hysterically, slapping his knees and splashing all around in the still-rising tide. Behind him stood the giant rocks of the jetty, and behind those, the black emptiness of the clouds and rain. When he saw that we were looking at him again, he straightened up and said, "See what I mean, Petey-Weety? You can't even fight like a man without your girlfriend helping you out. Oh well, I guess it's better for you that way." He paused briefly, his eyes sharped, and his voice got suddenly serious. "You were about to make me hurt you."

I remained calm but spoke firmly. "Derek, you have to leave us alone. All we want is to play on the beach and have a fun vacation. Can you please let us do that without any more trouble?"

He thought for a second. Thunder roared and another wave broke, this one really close. The ocean was all around us. "Well, Petey-Weety, what about what I want?" he answered. "I'm here for vacation, too. All I want is to knock down sandcastles, start fights, and throw people's favorite things into the ocean. I don't want to worry about some gutless punk and his precious fun. So, why don't *you* just leave *me* alone to do what I want, huh? Is that too . . . much . . . to . . . "

His voice trailed off and he stood perfectly still.

Through the rain I could tell his eyes had widened drastically, but it wasn't until the next lightning strike that I got a good look at his face. It was completely flushed, and his lips were quivering. He was clearly terrified by something.

He took a step back but met the jetty, and he reached his arms back to grasp the rock before he turned toward the beach and tried to run. But his legs didn't move, his body completely petrified by whatever horror he saw behind us. He looked back over our heads and let out a bloodcurdling scream. The three of us quickly turned around to see what it was, and until the day I die I will never forget what I saw there.

Towering over me, just inches away, was the tall, shadowy figure of a man. He was dressed in what looked like an old-timey military uniform, all gray, complete with a wide-brimmed hat and a riding cloak that was blowing like a cape in the wind. I searched for his eyes, but couldn't see them through the driving rain, and no lightning came to my aid this time. Yet I could tell he was looking at me; I could just *feel* it, his blank face staring deep into every part of me. And I wasn't scared at all.

I squeezed Sammy and Ali's hands, and they both stood fast without moving or saying a word. We just stood there in his presence, looking up at his shadowy face as the black gale blew all around us, and the waves beat down on the shore, and the furious rain continued to fall. But deep down I knew we were safe from the storm. Then he was gone.

I don't know how long we were standing there entranced by the apparition, but when we turned back around, Derek was nowhere to be found. The rain stopped, the howling wind slept, and the crashing waves relinquished their assault on the shore. Through the breaking clouds the last rays of sunlight led us home. We walked, still holding hands three abreast, each of us physically and emotionally spent, and each of us processing what had happened in our own way.

We encountered nothing and no one else on that walk home, except one thing. Just as we were turning toward our stairs, Sammy broke our rank and ran down to the water. I hadn't seen it, but when Sammy took off I scanned the beach and saw a little stuffed elephant gently flopping around in the waves.

Chapter 18

I WOKE UP EARLY THE NEXT MORNING, even before my parents. The sun was barely starting to peek up from behind the ocean. I tiptoed out of my room, went out to the front porch, and sat in a rocking chair. There was a cool breeze and the sound of the waves, but other than that, everything was silent and still.

It was Saturday. We had to be out of the rental house by 11 a.m. As soon as Mom got up, she'd start packing up our clothes, towels, and leftover kitchen stuff. Sammy and I would be in charge of stripping the sheets off all the beds and searching the house for misplaced toys and beach gear.

Dad would wander from room to room trying to look busy, even though his only job was to load up the car once everything was ready to go. Then we would all meet right out here and walk down to the beach together one last time, dip our feet in the warm Atlantic water, and let the sand cake our toes as we walked to the car for the drive home.

I sat there and immersed myself in the island. I felt the sun on my skin as it slowly gained the horizon, and let the heavy, salty air fill my lungs with every breath. In that moment I was more than the King of Pawleys. I closed my eyes and felt like I was *part* of Pawleys, like I just *belonged* there, no different from the jetties or the seashells or the sand.

"Pretty peaceful, huh, champ?"

I hadn't even heard him come outside, but when I looked over I saw Dad standing right beside my chair. He was still in his pajamas and was holding a cup of coffee. His hair was still all messed up from sleep, and he desperately needed to shave.

"Yes, sir," I said.

He took a sip of his coffee. "No matter how many times I come here, it never gets old. I mean, don't get me wrong—things change when you grow up. We gave you some extra privileges this week, but before long you'll be getting extra responsibilities, too. And just wait until you have kids of your own! The beach is a much different place when you have people depending on you for everything. And Pawleys is changing, too. The island is different now than when I was a kid, and I'm sure it'll be a little different next year, and the year after that. But there's just something about this place. . . . I don't know, it just always makes me feel at peace, no matter what's happening. Does that sound crazy? I mean, I've been coming here every summer for almost my entire life. Maybe I just don't know any different. Maybe it's just the *idea* of Pawleys, the vacation mentality, you know? Like I'd feel this way at any beach."

"No, you wouldn't," I replied simply. "And I wouldn't either. This place is special, Dad, and I finally understand the reasons why. I don't love it here because of the water or the sand. I love it because of our traditions—floating the creek, searching for Pawleys Shells, even eating those same meals every year. I love crabbing and exploring Myrtle Beach, and"—I hesitated— "watching for the Gray Man on stormy nights. I love it because . . . because you've taught me to love it. I could never feel that way about any other beach, or any other place, for that matter. No, this is our beach. This is our island."

Dad smiled. He closed his eyes and took a deep breath of ocean air. "Yeah," he said, and he sounded genuinely happy. He put his hand on my shoulder, looked me straight in the eyes, and said, "I love you, Pete."

"I love you, too, Dad." I got up and hugged him, and we stood there for one more moment together, absorbed by the sun and the sand and the sea.

Sammy came out and told us breakfast was ready, so we went inside and ate. As we started our chores, I realized something terrible, something I had never even considered but obviously should have seen coming.

I had to say goodbye to Ali today.

My stomach sank. It was all I could think of as we cleaned up the house and got ready for our departure. At one point I got fearful that her parents might be early risers and she may have already left, so I made my way to the kitchen window where I could see her driveway. The black SUV was still there, but a small collection of bags and beach chairs was sitting next to it, and just then Brian appeared and added a suitcase to the pile.

I ran to my parents' bedroom and found Dad folding some clothes. "Hey, Dad? Can I please take a break and go see Ali one last time? I, um, want to give her something."

"Okay, champ, just be back soon. I need your help bringing our stuff down to the car."

"Yes, sir," I answered. I raced to my room and grabbed

the rare memento I had found just three days ago, stuffed it into my pocket, and ran out the front door. I went down the stairs to the beach, did a U-turn back up to Ali's porch, and knocked on her door. Her mom answered.

"Hi, um, can Ali—"

But I was interrupted by Ali herself running past her mom and jumping into my arms. "Oh, Pete, I'm so glad you came over! I was really hoping we'd have a chance to say goodbye." She let go and turned to her mom, "Mom, can we please sit out here for just a few minutes? I'll be ready to go as soon as I come back in."

"Okay, but I'd like to say goodbye to Pete, too." She leaned down and hugged me almost as hard as Ali had. "It was so nice to meet you and your family this week. Thank you for playing with Ali and being such a good friend. And thank Sammy for me, too. Y'all have a safe trip home, okay?"

"Yes, ma'am," I said, and with a nod she was back behind the glass-panel door and closed it.

Ali and I sat down on the porch and faced each other. Our hands met, but neither of us spoke. I didn't know what to say, anyway. Only a week ago I had never met her, but we had been through so much that I felt like I had known her my whole life. She'd been nice to me, which was already more than I could say for a lot of the kids back home. But, of course, it was more than that. She'd laughed at my lame jokes. She'd helped me defeat my worst enemy. She'd brought me closer to my brother, and, even more impressive, helped me stand up to my dad. I felt my heart pounding in my chest and tears starting to form behind my eyes.

She was the first to speak. "Thank you, Pete. I don't know what I would have done this week without you. From the first time we met, you've been the kindest, most caring person I've ever known. You didn't have to help me or even hang out with me, but instead you pulled me through one of the scariest things that's ever happened to my family, and gave me a more amazing vacation than I could ever ask for. You showed me—"

"Stop," I interrupted. "Please, just stop." I could hear the quiver in my own voice. "This week hasn't been about me. I'm nothing, a nobody. But you made me feel like *somebody*. You gave me the confidence to stand up to Derek and my dad. I feel like I became a better person every day, every *hour* that I spent with you. All the way up to last night, in the storm, when—"

"Last night was the most incredible thing that's ever happened to me, and I'll remember it for the rest of my life."

We were silent again for a moment, both caught in sudden reflection of the wonder of the spectacle we witnessed. Then I remembered something.

"A second ago you mentioned the first time we met. Do you remember what you said when I asked you what you thought of Pawleys?"

She smiled.

"You said this place was magical. I guess you were more right than you realized."

"And a few days later, you told me that this place lives in every fiber of your being. Now I understand why."

It was all I could do to hold back my tears. I grabbed the shell from my pocket and held it out to her. "I found this the night we watched the sunset together. I want you to have it."

"Is this a Pawleys Island Shell?!"

I nodded, only then realizing she had never actually seen one before.

"Pete, I could never take this. It's precious to you."

"You're more precious to me than any shell, Ali." And with that, the tears burst though and began flowing freely down my face. Ali cried, too, and threw her arms around me, squeezing me so tight I could barely breathe. I returned her embrace, and we sat there crying on each other's shoulders for as long as it took. Finally, we loosened our arms, and as she pulled away she pressed her lips gently against my cheek.

That's not good enough, I thought, and quickly turned

my head toward her and met her lips with mine. It only lasted a second—one small, fleeting moment—but she immediately tightened her arms around me again, and we sat there holding each other for what felt like an eternity.

When we finally pulled back and locked eyes, we were both smiling. Through the tears I managed to let out a small giggle, and she returned in kind. My first kiss had come and gone, and the reality of the day sank back in. I knew it was time to say goodbye.

"Are you coming back next year?" I asked.

"I don't know. I've already told my parents that we should, but they haven't said anything yet."

The tears started fresh again. "Well, I guess this is goodbye."

"Yeah, I guess so."

We stood up and I took a deep breath. I gave her one more deep hug and one last quick kiss. Then I told her goodbye, she said the same, and we turned our separate ways. When I got to the bottom of her stairs I heard her open the door, so I looked back to catch one more glimpse of her. But I wasn't quick enough. All I could see was a bouquet of curly red hair collapsing into her mother's arms behind the glass door.

I tried to compose myself before walking back into our house, but I don't think I did a very good job. I dragged my heart heavily around the house as I helped Dad take our bags down to the driveway.

On my third trip, Ali's car was gone.

When we finished loading up, we threw our shoes and socks in the car and took our final walk down to the beach. It looked the same, but felt completely different. The island took hold of my very soul and was not about to let go, even as I climbed into the backseat and watched the ocean fade away behind me.

As we drove across the creek, I thought about everything there is in the world—all the places and all the people—and I couldn't begin to understand the way it worked out that one girl from some small town in Tennessee would just happen to take a vacation on *my* beach, at the same time I was there, and stay in the house right next door. It's like if two grains of sand on opposite sides of Pawleys somehow, against all odds, met up and had a wild adventure together that made them feel like they were more than just sand.

Epilogue

I steer my minivan onto the South Causeway and feel my heartbeat speeding up and goose bumps forming all over my arms. Even after all these years, I still have the same involuntary reaction when we get this close. Then, all of a sudden, the trees give way to marshes, and spread out in front of us is my favorite place in the whole world.

Pawleys Island.

Unable to control themselves, my son and daughter start doing their "Awesome Dance" in the backseat, a hilarious ritual they invented a few years ago. They've tried teaching it to me, but apparently my failures are more hysterical than the dance itself. I glance over and see my wife smiling in the passenger seat; I grab her hand and give it a squeeze, and as we cross over the creek I feel a wave of calming comfort wash over me. This place just . . . envelopes me, like I'm a part of it that's been missing for the last fifty-one weeks and finally made the island whole again with my return.

Of course, I can never be here without thinking of that summer. Every detail lives permanently ingrained in my memory, from that horrifying first night, to the thrilling view of my kingdom from the top of the dunes, to our stupid, juvenile tricks in Myrtle Beach, and everything in between.

And by my side, through it all, was Ali.

I remember her sand-covered hand waving to me on the first day, before we even met. I remember falling asleep on the couch together—completely by accident—our bodies sticky with sweat and reeking of sunscreen. I remember her curly red hair dancing in the breeze as we held hands for the first time. And I remember the fire in her rain-soaked eyes when she spun me around and lowered my hands to my sides, just before our gray friend appeared. She was perfect, and together we were the masters of Pawleys Island, arrogantly shabby, and no one could ever dethrone us.

But that was a long time ago now. These days, my time

at the beach is spent cooking and cleaning, chatting with the neighbors, and making runs to the grocery store. Sure, I still search for Pawleys Shells, float the creek, and eat the same exact meals as always. But the fun part now is passing all of those traditions along to my children, watching them do all of the same things I used to do when I was a kid on this tiny island.

I just hope they learn to love it as much as I do.

"Pete, are you going to yell at her?"

I look over at my wife and then shoot a glance at the kids through the mirror. Their eyes look frightened, like when they know they're in trouble. "Um, why, what happened?" I honestly don't even know.

"Your daughter refused to share her juice and it got spilled all over the back seat. Didn't you hear them arguing?"

"I guess I, uh . . . kids, you're going to clean that up, you hear me?"

"Yes, sir," they reply in unison, and I can hear the surprise in their voices. I let them off easy. Hey, we're on vacation, right?

I unlock the automatic doors as we pull into the driveway, and as soon as the car stops we all jump out and bolt to the ocean. My wife hangs back to grab the beach bag out of the trunk without even asking me to help. She knows better than to hold me back.

As my bare feet touch the sand, I remember sitting on the front porch of this same house, thinking for the first time that I was a part of Pawleys. I was right. It's the same feeling I just had five minutes ago when we crossed the bridge. But what I didn't understand back then was that the opposite was true as well: Pawleys was a part of me.

And it still is.

And it always will be.

THE END

Acknowledgments

This book would never have been written if not for my grandmother, Laddie, who started many of the traditions included in this story, and my parents, who instilled in me the love and family values I have attempted to portray. Thanks go out to all my Pawleys playmates through the years: Doran, Bart, Beautiful Aunt Judy, Ryan, Liz, and the new generation: JB, Ben, Drew, Sam, and Ruthie. Special love to Jay, my partner in crime ever since you's been born, and of course Trisha, for supporting me through every step of this journey and all the journeys yet to come. I love y'all!

Finally, thanks to the awesome staff at Lanier Press for making this dream of mine a reality, and to my illustrator, Maryia Kapitsa, for more amazing cover art than I could have ever imagined.

About the Author

David Bernstein is a lifelong Pawleys vacationer and a lover of hammocks, crabbing, and all things Arrogantly Shabby. He lives in Georgia with his wife and three sons. *The King of Pawleys* is his first novel.